The Flying Island

Also by Romana Petri

Other People's Fathers
An Umbrian War

Romana Petri

THE FLYING ISLAND

TRANSLATED BY
Sharon Wood

The Toby Press

First English Language Edition 2002

The Toby Press LLC
www.tobypress.com

Originally published as *La donna delle Azzorre*

Copyright © Romana Petri, 2001

Translation copyright © Sharon Wood, 2002

ISBN 1 902881 64 8, *paperback*

A CIP catalogue record for this title is available from the British Library

Designed by Breton Jones, London

Original cover photography by Robert Wheeler

Typeset in Garamond by Jerusalem Typesetting

Printed and bound in the United States by
Thomson-Shore Inc., Michigan

to João Freitas,
most faithful of husbands

Contents

Chapter one *Pico*, 1

Chapter two *João Freitas*, 5

Chapter three *Julio Neves*, 23

Chapter four *Maria Moniz*, 37

Chapter five *Malvina Sebastião*, 45

Chapter six *Drink*, 53

Chapter seven *Isabel and Maria José Lima*, 63

Chapter eight *João Vieira Freitas*, 73

Chapter nine *Cabrito*, 83

Chapter ten *Arcos*, 95

Pico

The sky is covered with clouds that seem rapidly to melt into each other but are separate, overlapping each other in parallel streaks. It's because of the wind, shifting them softly at will; they slip away while down below we stand with our arms crossed, holding our shirts tight against us.

It was on a day such as this, with the sky in constant motion and clouds scurrying across the tip of Mount Pico, that I met João Freitas. He was walking along the main street of Arcos, a red earth track that seemed to magnify the heat of the sun, burning up its rays the moment the wind dropped even for an instant. He was coming along slowly and the first thing I noticed about him was his blue cap with the slogan *Azores Concrete—All Kinds of Cement Work.* Even before shaking my hand he pointed out to me the low flight of a seagull and smiled his open, ingenuous smile, like someone showing off to a tourist the prodigious nature of his wonderful land.

I had arrived in Pico the evening before, after an exhausting journey. The weather was verging on the autumnal—the island covered with slanting rain from which no umbrella could protect you.

I

Signora Maria Silva had come to meet me at Port Madalena. We had been put in touch by a mutual friend, and over the winter we'd spoken several times by phone. Stilted conversations, given the language problems, not to mention the unsettling hum of the echo, which always lingers around voices which have an ocean between them. We came to an agreement, in the mystery of those slow and repeated phrases; she described her house near the sea, in just the part that I wanted, Cabrito. I told her as best I could that I would rent it at the very reasonable price of eighty thousand escudos a month.

But things are always different from far off, and perhaps I had misunderstood, because when Maria Silva took me to her house in Cabrito she explained that there was neither water nor electricity, and to have either I had to activate a rusty old generator that seemed on the point of exploding every time it was switched on. But even then the light was feeble and the water trickled down so slowly that it didn't even make a noise—*agua fraca*.

While this was serious enough but not catastrophic, the real problem was that even though the house was no more than fifty metres from the sea, you couldn't see it because of a dry stone wall that had been built at the front, goodness knows why. I didn't have the heart to say anything to her, and I spent my first night in Pico in that house, giving up on the generator and lighting the two solitary candles I found in a drawer. After dinner I went to sit in the dark of the patio, listening to the mournful cries of the *cagarros* swooping down, thinking they looked rather like seagulls, only larger, with their large, dull white forms, wings outspread; and looking at the faint light from the only house to be seen in the darkness that swallowed up every outline and shape. I couldn't see the ocean but luckily I could hear it, and after trying to read a little by candlelight this at least helped me drop off to sleep. In the morning I was woken by Maria Silva, come to bring me a basin of fresh milk and some *pão doce*.

Here people are really kind, in a way that we are quite unused to in our own lands. We sat down to eat together, talking as best we could, and it was beyond me to lie to her. I told her in all honesty that I couldn't stay in that house where I could cope with *não luz publica, não agua,* but I couldn't bear the thought of having come almost ten thousand kilometres to end up without a view of the sea. Maria Silva threw up her arms, holding in one hand a slice of *pão doce* which she had already dipped in her milk, and said I was right, that she'd always missed the sea there too, even though she was born and bred on the island and could see it all the time. She knew I came from Italy, but wasn't Italy that long strip of land which stuck right out into the sea? Into the sea, certainly, but that didn't mean everyone could see it. What a shame, she said, her arms back down in her lap, and since she was really very kind, she added that we could sort something out. If I wasn't too tired from the trip we could walk over to Arcos, her cousin who was an emigrant who came back now and then from California and who had two houses right by the sea, with electricity and plentiful running water. Although he was there this year with his family perhaps he didn't need both of them. I agreed, but on one condition, that I should pay her for her trouble, for all those months of complicated arrangements, a third of those eighty thousand escudos for my word which I had given to her. She made a gesture which I couldn't describe, waving a hand in the air almost as though she were drawing a picture, and said something without bothering to make herself understood, as if talking to someone who spoke the same language and grasped every subtle nuance. Then she got up to wash the cups and tidy up the few things that I had touched. When she had finished she said: Let's go straight away, my cousin gets back from his walk about now.

I hadn't noticed it the day before, perhaps because of the bad weather, but now that the sun was out I saw a landscape of rare beauty, an almost fiery earth set afloat in the ocean as if for a game. We walked almost half an hour, then Maria Silva sat down on a low circular wall by a deep well of lava stone where a metal cup, tied with string, knocked against the edge in the wind. It's drinking water, she told me. Slightly salty, but good. My cousin will come by this way, he won't be long.

I can't remember much of what I was thinking at that

moment; I was looking at the well that seemed to rest first against the sea and then against the dark horizon, standing out against the strong blue of the sky. I pulled my jacket around me against the wind, and in the distance I saw João Freitas coming towards us.

Chapter two

João Freitas

From his appearance you would have said he was an old man, but he couldn't have been more than sixty-five. Sometimes work does that to people, I thought, especially those who leave to labour far away from their own land. In the case of João Freitas it was also the drink: here in the Azores, *licor de amora* and *angelica*, in far-off California beer and cheap whisky. He had the puffy, child-like cheeks of alcoholics, light blue bags beneath his eyes crisscrossed by thousands of sharp, tiny wrinkles. He asked me if I would prefer him to speak in English or Portuguese. I should have answered in English, because I had studied it for so many years, but I felt strangely ashamed, it seemed to me a discourtesy to make him speak the language of his work place here, in his own land. I would prefer Portuguese, I said, but please speak slowly, *devagar*.

Since his voice was soft he came up close to me, to tell me what his house was like. I asked if it was far from where we were, and he pointed it out with the barest tilt of his chin because it was the one right in front of us. But he made no move to go over there and carried on describing it to me, sitting next to us on the little wall by the well, so close I could smell the bitter breath of years of drinking bouts, while Maria Silva listened in silence and rubbed the hem of her petticoat. João Freitas would often stop speaking to smile loudly, a gesture which filled me with melancholy because these were the only moments when I was aware of his years in America, that manner of filling silences with noisy smiles which everyone learns over there.

It seemed strange to me to be talking about a house which was right in front of us, but perhaps he liked to do things slowly, to consume time, feel it, and so rediscover the habits of the island. Then at last he got up, and shrugging his shoulders with a smile that flashed back to his long lost youth, he said, I don't know if you will like it, it's an antique house, with many antique things in it.

I was taken aback to discover that the meaning of the word antique, was here very different from the meaning it usually has for us—a rare object of luxury for those who can afford it, almost always appreciated for its value. Here, antique signified not modern, something which has existed for a long time and which it has never occurred to anyone to replace. This was the original meaning of the word, which we have replaced with the word old.

It was a lovely house, very plain, with its dark wooden beds and single wardrobe. Apart from the bathroom, the rooms were divided by coloured curtains, and the main door was closed from the inside by a green, painted latch. How long are you thinking of staying, he asked me. A month, maybe two, I don't know yet. He replied, all right then, and went off, telling me he would be back straight away with sheets and some pots and pans. Maria Silva waited until he had gone to say goodbye to me and then she set off too, happy for the way she had managed to sort things out and without the least regret for the lost rent. She gave me an affectionate hug and wished me good luck. *Auguri!*

I was alone in the house, the sea was nearby, I could see it, but I didn't stand to watch it because in the kitchen I had noticed three framed photographs hung in a diagonal line along one wall. In the first, the highest one, were a man and a woman who must have been sixty years old. It was one of those photos of bygone days, slightly touched up by the photographer. A lovely clear close-up of their faces, both of them with their hair neatly brushed, and smiling. It could have been taken on one of their wedding anniversaries. One thing I couldn't make out, whether the woman had a fine necklace or if the circular mark around her neck was a perfect wrinkle, or the cut from an old operation, which had never quite healed properly. Not only must it have been taken by a photographer, but he must have done it in his studio, because the background was the clear monochrome of a photographer's screen. On the left, the ingenuous hand of a decorator had painted an indoor plant.

The second photograph must have been from more or less the same period, because the couple was not much changed; two or three years might have gone by, maybe, no more. This time the photograph was full-length and with them were their children, three boys and a girl, two next to the mother and two next to the father. They were all standing and here, too, you could see the work of the photographer because they were all standing in an unnatural pose, three turned towards the left and three towards the right, but all with their heads turned to face the camera, and as you looked at them you could almost feel the painful pulling of their neck muscles. Judging from the way they were dressed it could have been the Sixties, but here time must have gone by rather differently, fashion was not as ephemeral as elsewhere. Whatever, this must have been a special occasion too. In the third photo, on the other hand, a good amount of time had clearly passed, at least fifteen years, maybe as many as twenty. The couple were still in the centre of the photo; time had made both of them rather thinner. This was why they seemed sadder, when in fact it was only old age. Now I understood why the man in the other photographs had a strangely light circle around his eyes compared to the rest of his face—he wore glasses and took them off to be photographed. He didn't do that any more, his eyesight was failing, he wouldn't have even known where to look, and anyway he was no longer concerned to look his very best. Old age brings with it a certain need for realism, for no more illusions.

They were sitting on a blue sofa. Behind them there was an immense panoramic photograph of the islands of Pico and Faial, which face each other. This made me think that the third photograph had been taken in America, and this time by someone in the family. The pair were surrounded by eight grandchildren, washed and scrubbed for the picture, yet strangely enough they all looked roughly the same age, somewhere between six and eight. In the eyes of each of them, if only you could read them, was written their destiny. I couldn't say why but seen like that, in the past, with a future that had already happened, they made you enormously sad.

Unite and multiply, man was told. And the two of them, if you totted it up, had done just that. Literally.

It's my uncle's family on my mother's side, João Freitas told me, as he came back into the house.

I thought it was yours, I replied. Isn't this house yours?

Certainly it's mine but my cousin comes here for his holidays. He's that boy there in the photograph, he said, pointing him out.

Does he live in America too?

Yes, California. He's the one who put these pictures up.

And isn't he coming this year? No, not this year, too much money to come down here with his whole family. They don't come every year. I've brought you some sheets and towels, some pots and pans. Plates and glasses are already here and you will find blankets in that trunk.

I still have my luggage in Maria Silva's house, I said, she told me to leave the key under a flowerpot.

I'll take you in the car. Afterwards, when you've settled in you can come to my house for a glass of *angelica*, which I made myself. I'll introduce you to my family.

It's not that I forgot João Freitas' invitation; it's just that I was taking my time, I was looking around and breathing in the smell of the house. You don't go in where others have lived without feeling a certain sense of embarrassment. Time stretches out, we pick up an object and we don't know where to put it, we change its place, it's always been ours but now it doesn't belong to us quite so much, it's trying to fit into the house and in this way, now, late on, it starts to belong to everyone else who has been here too.

I decided that I didn't really feel like unpacking and went out onto the patio to the few metres of lava rock that separated me from the sea. You just need rubber shoes and you can walk on it like a cat, almost more attached to the ground than along any normal smooth road. It's the effect of the basalt vomited up by the eruption of the volcano, boiling away who knows how many hundreds of years in the guts of the earth and then spewed out in flowing lava as far down as the sea. It's the rocks' nostalgic yearning for a return to the depths, which keeps us so solid on the rock. As I was thinking this, I had already crossed those few metres and I was sitting on the rocks looking at the sea which looked calm enough from the house but which here smashed violently against the rock face, throwing up great sprays of water which evaporated into an invisible cloud even though I could feel it on my skin. There was no other sound. Any other sound was as if behind a thick plate of glass. Gone, too, was the mournful cry of the seagulls which seemed to be flying silently, or perhaps they really were silent, stunned by the crashing of the waves, which opened up into a mass of white spray.

Neither did I hear João Freitas, and I don't even know how long he stood there calling me because I caught sight of him by chance, turning round to have a look at the house from this angle, and saw him, waving his hat with *Azores Concrete* on it in his right hand. I couldn't hear him but he was almost certainly shouting too. The wind was so strong I had to hold my hair back with my hands in order to see where to put my feet, and as I came up to him, my over-riding feeling was of a sort of fraternal pity for João Freitas. However, I told myself that I was forever attributing grief, that terrible way I have of reading it in the hearts of others. And this time it was the fact that he was coming back from a country which was not his, that heart-wrenching *Azores Concrete—All Kinds of Cement Work,* going

over there to breathe cement dust, obeying the orders of others, and
then, saving up after goodness knows how many sacrifices, finally
setting up on his own with the name of his own archipelago, so that
at least the name would remind him of where he was born, but carrying on just the same, breathing in cement dust in a foreign land.
You have some strange ideas, I said to myself, perhaps he's happy
this way and every time he comes back he's changed just a little bit
more, just as objects do, belonging less and less to Pico and more
and more to California.

As I came up to him, he was just a short man who stretched
out his hand to help me over the last couple of metres, in a gesture
as ancient and chivalric as his stone house.

You should be careful staying out in all this wind, he told me,
it can do you no good if you are not used to it.

It didn't occur to me to tell him that I already knew the
Azores. I followed him lightly, crossing over the reddish road with
him, and from the lucid world of the living I felt as if I was entering
the opaque world of the dead.

Where I come from back in Italy, the ground floor of a house
is almost always divided into a sitting room, which takes up most of
the space, a kitchen and a small bathroom. In Umbria, too, where I
live, the rooms which once upon a time had been used for housing
animals are now called *tavernette*, and there is not even the slightest lingering smell of what they once were. Here it's different: the
ground floor is a single, large, workroom where people cook in the
summer because it's cooler. It's used as a laundry, they hang out the
clothes here when it rains, it's the place where they keep enormous
onions and tiny potatoes all absolutely identical, the demijohns of
vinho de chiero and those of *angelica*, a special liqueur, a strange mixture of *aguardente* and wine, which everybody makes in their own
home and offers to visitors at any time of the day. If anybody were to
say to these people that they are wasting space they would just smile
and reply in astonishment that that is just the way their house is.

I met the family of João Freitas in this great space of his lovely
house. His sister Fernanda was peeling and cutting a mountain of

potatoes that she was going to fry for their dinner. She was helped by a beautiful girl with a South American looking face, with two enormous eyes the colour of glistening black velvet. Their beauty was so different it seemed impossible they could be mother and daughter, but so it was. In my thoughts I wished her to stay exactly as she was for as long as possible, with such vehemence that though she didn't know it, I'm sure I put a spell on her. If I were to meet her again after twenty or thirty years, I'm sure I would find her just the same as I saw her then. The son of João Freitas was lying in a hammock that groaned with the rocking motion, which had just got him off to sleep and almost touched the ground with his great weight. He looked at least thirty-five to me but in fact was only twenty-four. The heavy sleep of Paul the pachyderm, American from head to toe, not just by name. His swimming trunks were still damp on his thighs, brightly coloured Bermudas which when dry must have puffed out like a skirt. He gave off a strange smell, a mixture of deodorant, which slowly, as he slept, gave way to a naturally more fetid odour.

You shouldn't have let him be born over there, I wished I could say to João Freitas. Perhaps you couldn't help it, but all the same it's your fault. That must be why so many Americans are obese, they have a great thirst in their soul, which has been carried off to where it should never have gone, and they make up for the grief of the move by drowning their food in strangely coloured sauces. All the fat which your fathers used up in your sorrowful memories has been taken over by them; each time you sigh, a deposit of blubber unfurls like a slice of bacon around their children's bodies to soften the blow. Now Paul was snoring loudly, I passed by him and saw his tiny mouth in all that face, a half open mouth, a tiny little hole where there was nothing but darkness. His wife Norma, a minute Mexican woman, watched him sleep as she sang a lullaby to their little two-year old daughter. I wondered what they were like in bed, how they expressed their feelings in a language they had both adopted in order to understand one another. Maybe he didn't, but she would certainly translate everything simultaneously into Spanish to feel more warmth from the words: *I love you—te quiero.* Perhaps they don't even talk, he out of exhaustion and she following his lead. This was their first child; soon there would be others to take more words away.

You have a lovely family.

Yes, very. I didn't even know they were coming. They gave me a surprise, ten days after I had arrived here. But let's go upstairs now, I want to show you the photographs and offer you a glass of my own *angelica.* If you like it, I will give you a bottle, because you won't find nothing around here as good as mine. Nothing—anything—I never could work out the difference, I've never studied English, just repeated it like a parrot, and that's not so very different from what we do all our lives, is it? We learn by watching and listening, and those who get on best are the ones who have the courage to show their mistakes.

As he said this, he showed me out of the room and walked in front of me up the steep, uneven steps outside the house, with the sun by now the colour of oranges, ready to drown in the ocean for the whole sad duration of a night without light. This is what disturbs the waters when we feel them in our sleep, and this is also what warms them, sweetening our nightly dreams. As we went up the steps, I clearly heard João Freitas' first, long sigh, and it was not because he was tired from the physical effort.

He didn't take his cap off inside the house either, so tied was he to his work and grateful enough to think of himself as a client when he looked in the mirror: Who knows, it's good to know, I'll make a note of the name and address. These are little American games he plays, he must have acted out that little scene a thousand times, seen it when he was still an employee and then finally done it himself when he became boss of *Azores Concrete,* at the Christmas dinner for the men who worked for him. They don't laugh to be polite down there, they laugh for real. But now he was returning to his old habits, and before pouring me a glass of *angelica,* he washed and rewashed the glass in a basin as a sign of hospitality. Almost mystical gestures, the same as those of the priest before his flock, after drinking from the chalice the blood of Christ so uselessly spilled.

—Do you like it?

—It's excellent.

—Then you must have a bottle as a mark of friendship. It was already decided.

Then his face turned dark, much darker than his unshaven beard. It didn't take much now, only a drop, and he waved towards a room with his hand: go and have a look inside and then tell me if you like it. And to listen to his sigh it was as if his lungs were inside there. Perhaps it would have been normal to ask why he wanted to talk about it to me in particular, if he would have done the same with anyone else who had rented his house. But this was a question that remained unanswered and was destined to remain so, as I never uttered it. Inside there was a creaseless bed covered in crocheted lace, and on the bed a pedestal of white painted wood, and on the pedestal a statue of *Bom Jesus Milagroso,* at least three feet high. What I remember about it now is different from what I thought at the time. Then I was just surprised and embarrassed, not just because it wasn't what I was expecting but because of how different that statue was from all the others, or perhaps it would be more accurate to say from the statues we usually see in our churches. At the time, I was struck by a wig with long curls down to its shoulders. It brought to mind the mannequins I used to see when I was a little girl in men's clothes shops, but this one looked like a mannequin dressed up as the son of God and thus struck me as more than a little ridiculous. Now I realise that its beauty was in its joyfulness and great purity; in the conviction somehow produced by that piece of coloured gesso in whoever looked at it, making it possible for them to recognise Christ without any bewilderment—without the intercession of anything otherworldly and yet much that was human. It seemed like something that might come to life at any moment. It was a lovely statue, with an elegant tunic of white linen and a red, gold-trimmed cloak. Pinned onto the breast was a plastic heart dripping with blood. Even today I am moved by the thought of whoever sewed those sacred clothes, knowing for whom they were destined.

I closed the door behind me again and said: It's very beautiful.

João Freitas poured me another glass of *angelica*, and without a glance either at me or at the door, which I had shut, he asked: Do you believe in miracles?

There are questions which make us smile out of place, out of a sudden sense of shame. I would like to have answered that I believed in them, but my voice remained locked up in my mind, and my arms came away slightly from my body, like one who does not know what to say. At times we are outside of time, we remain balanced in a neutral moment, which goes neither backwards nor forwards. This is the strange time of permanence, the time which happens to us just rarely in our lifetimes, when we feel as if we have lost the past yet have no future, and we feel we have found great peace. Every experience tells its own story, but mine tells me that we were both helped greatly by the fact that we spoke two different tongues and found ourselves in a country that really was *milagroso*.

Five months ago, in California, my wife died of breast cancer, said João Freitas. As was his habit, he repeated this information spontaneously, but not in American this time, he said it twice in Portuguese, and the stress fell on the word *murreu*, the most tragic word in the world, the only one which contains within its sound the pain of the one who abandons this earth as well as of the one left behind to grieve alone. He said it twice and with his hand he made the gesture of crushing his chest.

She died three years after the operation and when she really was on the point of dying she would call those years a mutilated illusion. Would you believe me if I told you that she was beautiful even without her two breasts. I didn't say it to make her feel better, it was absolutely true. Maybe it was because she didn't hide herself. She would come out of the bathroom with her towel tied around her hips, showing off the glory of those two scars on her chest like a warrior's wounds. We had met at the procession of *Sam Mateus*, on a day so hot I can't remember another one like it. Later, when everything was decided, she would make a joke about it, she used to say I had set that day alight with the flames of my passion. I saw her walking barefoot like the faithful, like those utterly devoted to the statue of *Bom Jesus Milagroso*, which on that day of the year is carried out of the church and around the village on the shoulders of six strong men. She walked holding a lighted candle, which dripped wax on her hand, but her face didn't betray any signs of pain. I saw her face later because she was wearing a veil. What struck me above all were those feet and her hand melted into the wax. At the time you had to get on with things quickly around here, you couldn't just eye up a girl for any length of time, you had to make your intentions clear to the family. To do that I wore my dead father's decent suit, which my mother had altered to fit the size I was then. Talking about it like this, you'd think I was already a grown man, but I was only sixteen years old. I worked as a fisherman with my brothers, and we had our own boat. Things went as was the custom in those days, she and her mother appeared only for a moment, when they brought in the bottle of *aguardente de bagaco*, which I drank with her father and her brothers. It all lasted as long as it took the sun to set and then I went home on foot as the first night fell. My mother was waiting for me along the road, this Arcos road here, a thin woman always dressed in mourning. Well then, she said, are they giving her to you? I nodded yes and that evening I didn't eat my dinner, I told her to cover it for me for the next day and I went to bed with my stomach full of that liqueur and my head whirling with dreams. Real feeling needs few words and knows that facts can wait. We went on in this way until we were interrupted by the war—training on Terceira island and then off to Angola. A stupid, cruel war, which I never understood. But I would have thought the same thing of any war; it's the view of a working man who in war just sees his time being wasted. Don't mind me, I'm a pacifist by nature, and experience in life can lead you to conclusions which are inevitably very personal. As far as I'm concerned, when you pile horror onto horror there's nothing left to understand. When I came back I knew she had waited for me like an honest woman.

We thought long and hard about what we should do, and perhaps it was the experience of war still in me, I thought that here in our country, or rather in the Portuguese world, everything would drag out for a long time, I was afraid that out of that war would come another one, and so once we were married we went to California, which seemed to me a land far enough away. You can see the photo of our wedding up there by the chimney. We were young then. And I have to admit that that's where everything starts and everything finishes, there's not much to tell about California, just work and a bit of money put aside, nothing to say. Our children were born there. They can speak Portuguese of course, but amongst themselves they just speak English. Sad, isn't it? They have a real American accent and I will have a foreigner's accent for the rest of my life. Over there the Portuguese stick close together, but don't think badly of us and don't be offended, because with us it wasn't like with you Italians. We are simple people, only a handful emigrate to other countries in Europe, we live beside the clear transparency of the sea, us islanders and the mainlanders too, we don't look behind us. It's because we are simple that we are very honest. We like great parties, so big that we have to hire a hall just to get three families together. You can see the last one in that photo hanging on the wall opposite you. I've kept all of them. But I only hung up the last one. One of these days, if you would like, I'll get my glasses on and show you all those who are dead now. I don't need glasses for just one person, and if that was the last party it was because she was the one who organised them, every year with the same impatience. Do you know what they were like, those parties? They were perfect, where at the end everyone went away happy, and everyone said the same thing: Thelma, every year you give us the gift of a return to Pico without having to pay for a ticket. And she was bright and cheerful right to the end, only when we went home did she feel upset. That was the last party; if you look at the photo you can see her laughing like all the others who didn't know they were going to die even though they were already old. But she already had those warrior's scars on her breast.

João Freitas fell silent and contemplated his glass of *angelica*. This must be the consolation of a heavy drinker, pausing to look at the bottom of the glass, and like a God who judges evil, condemning all pain to death. And the level has to be constant, a real drinker has to leave a finger of alcohol in the glass even if he decides he's going to drink no more that day, otherwise the pain will not drown and he's developing cirrhosis for nothing.

I took advantage of his silence to look closely at the photo. There must have been at least two hundred people, and what I got from it was a very sad feeling. It made me feel very sad. Thelma, every year you make us the gift of a return to Pico, here in this hall, green lino on the floor, all of them horribly dressed, there's nobody who dresses like that here in Pico. That's what it means, I thought, to go off as emigrants to the other side of the world, it comes down to this. I turned my gaze elsewhere, on a much older image, the one of their wedding, which had taken place in Pico. That lovely way of being when you were different, and not just because it was a black and white photo, the texture of the paper roughened by the sun, season after season, over the years. It's that each of us is more authentic before we undergo transformations. If we apply it to others this was a banal enough thought, but do we ever notice it in ourselves? Certainly João Freitas would have been bemused if I'd said to him, in this one you are yourselves, while here you are different people. Perhaps he would have replied that that was the longest period of their lives, putting quantity on the other side of the scales. But I would have been the only one to understand where the pointer was really indicating. He gave another sigh, a long one with much restrained despair in it, the sound accompanied by the sloshing of another glass being poured for me and for himself.

It happened after she died, he said, speaking softly. I lost all my faith. I would say it's human even though it's shameful; but it's inhuman not to be terrified when it happens. I changed a lot, I became a man without respect, I started to look about me, to look at living people who were her age or even older and to think, what have you got that she didn't have, why have you outlasted her? This is the fast track away from faith, putting yourself in the place of the Lord, like an ordinary citizen who opens up his newspaper and blasts a decision made by the government; he shakes his head, says what he thinks and thinks he's wise, and is astonished that those people so far above him haven't come to the same conclusion. But to do that to God means siding with his enemy, the devil, giving in to its voice, giving him your soul and your blood.

Maybe you think I'm crazy, but I didn't sleep that night because sleep had gone away together with her death, and I didn't even have the heart to stretch out in that bed which had become so cold. You are young and so perhaps you don't know it yet, but there is in life an attachment which as time goes on becomes tighter and tighter like a metal band, and the further away from your youth you move, the stronger it gets. The two of us used to call it the touch of your body, because it's no longer even an embrace, it's the habit you have when you've slept with one person for your whole life, to lie down side by side with the other before you go to sleep, putting the warmth of your two bodies together. And to go to sleep peacefully all you need from the body lying next to you is the slightest touch, the curl of an elbow or the softer touch of a thigh. A couple which has lasted shows itself when it goes to bed; the person who goes to sleep while the other one is still fiddling around in the house has not only become old, but has also forgotten his youth. After she died, I would spend whole nights in the armchair, without even dozing off. If I did ever nod off it was during the day, in full light, the light that alleviates exhaustion just a little. It happened one of those nights, and it wasn't even dark. She came into the room opening the door; I saw her walk and sit down opposite me just as she did when she was alive. She wore the clothes she had been buried in—a grey wool winter dress—and I don't know how but I could see her body too, as if it were naked, and more than anything else I could clearly see the two scars where her breasts had been. She said to me, why do you give me such pain? It was you who caused me this grief by dying, I answered her.

It's life, she said, things happen as they must happen; men go around clouded with illusions. All that treatment was useless, a waste of time. If you are going to survive a serious illness you will do it without all that treatment. I said to her that we couldn't know that, and she answered, I know, and that's why we sacrificed so much. Listen João, if you ever fall ill don't waste time like I did, however long you have left to live just live for the best.

You were the best, I told her. If I were to fall ill I wouldn't know what to choose. Then come over here by me, she said, come here and hold me.

Can we do that? I asked. I don't know João, but I would really like to try.

And that's what we did, whether you believe me or not, an embrace which was not solid but very scented, and then I remembered that it was because when she died I poured onto her dress all the perfume she had left in her bottle, because they say death gives off a bad smell and I didn't want that for her. After that embrace she rested her head on my shoulder and said, smiling: The touch of your body, I hadn't felt that for a while.

I asked her, Did you miss it? A little, but I hope that will pass soon.

For me it will never pass, I told her. It's different, you are still alive. But listen to me now, I didn't come here just to embrace you, because if you really want to know the dead can do this whenever they wish, they don't have to show themselves, and you feel as if someone has brushed lightly past you, you pass your hand through your hair and say it must have been the wind. What I want to say to you is that I don't like the way in which you have taken my death. You've changed, you've turned into a bitter soul of a man who no longer believes in eternal justice. One thing you people still alive should get through your heads—staying a bit longer than someone else on the face of the earth is not a privilege, the choices aren't made that way, there is a much wider design which has nothing to do with good or bad deeds. I won't explain because you wouldn't understand it, you can only understand when you're dead and you are still in your time of ignorance. But the man of faith knows that the length of a life means nothing, he doesn't know why but he knows this is not the point. I would like you to go back to being the man you were when I met you, because otherwise I will have to tell you something you will not like.

What? I asked her.

That if I were alive and met you now, I would not marry you.

Really?

Really.

Tell me what I should do then.

Well, how long is it since you've been to Pico?

Almost four years. You got sick, we went from one doctor to the next, then the operation, the treatment…

I know, I know, all that time thrown away. Listen, I'm not saying that once you're dead you know how things might have been, but know this, maybe if we'd gone back to Pico, with that wonderful wind you always find there, and the islands of São Jorge and Faial which we could see from our house, who knows, maybe I would have got better there.

Please Thelma, please don't say that.

Listen to me João, even though I'm dead, I need you to go back to what you were before, to go back to Pico whether you want to or not, start again from where it all began.

What do you mean?

I mean the *Bom Jesus Milagroso*, I need a statue like the one standing in the *Sam Mateus* church, smaller but otherwise the same, I want it on our bed over there, and every year on the day of the procession you will be at Pico and you will carry it on your shoulder, saying a prayer for me, the prayer for the dead, and for your own ungrateful soul. Only in this way will you turn back into the man I left behind me on earth. Promise me you will do it.

I will do it, I said to her, but then I was overcome by a sudden fear.

How will I know, I asked her, if you are happy?

Do you know what, she started to laugh. She laughed like a woman still alive, with warm blood running through her body, and if her breasts had still been there I would have seen them shaking. When she calmed down she put a hand lightly on my leg and said, souls that are happy have no need to come back to the earth. If you never see me again you will know I am happy.

Then she became serious and I realised our time together was coming to an end. She got to her feet, her body luminously transparent, and headed for the door. Before opening it, she turned back to me once more and spoke to me with a voice that was already far away. One last thing, she said to me, but this is just to satisfy me, because I know the answer already, but you were always a man of few words, and towards the end we didn't even have time for that. Tell me now.

What? I asked her.

That you loved me. I want you to tell me.

Yes, I loved you. Very, very much.

She said goodbye with a rapid movement of her hand and an almost girlish smile, then she opened the door, closed it quietly behind her and I heard her steps in the hallway, the same steps as all those years we had spent together, the same as when she sometimes went out alone.

I expected João Freitas to sigh, but instead he swallowed down the *angelica* still left in his glass and recorked the bottle. Then he disappeared, and came back almost immediately with an ice cube tray still in its cellophane wrapping.

For you, he said, you will need it.

But there are already two in the fridge, I said.

I know, but you can't have too many of them, when the wind dies down it's terribly hot here.

Thank you so much, but I won't even use the ones I already have. I never drink anything iced.

Really?

Certainly, I don't want any problems with my stomach.

Who put such nonsense into your head? All the doctors say the same thing; ask any of them.

Must be those Italian doctors, he told me, old-fashioned. In America, even the children know that ice never hurt anyone, far from it, it's good for you.

Chapter three

Julio Neves

I n the beginning we're never happy with anything, that's normal, it's part of getting used to a new set of habits, which is always hard work. We set off with the desire to find something different, and to start with, we do everything we can to recreate what we left behind. It's a contradiction inherent in that section of humanity that is accustomed to leaving not out of need, but out of restlessness of spirit.

This is why, after just a few days, I felt the sudden urgent need to change house again. I walked as far as Santa Luzia and waited for the bus to Madalena, where I hired a car for a day. It doesn't take much to get around the whole island; it can't be more than a hundred kilometres. I had decided to see the whole coast, but instead I stopped at Prainha. I arrived there quite by chance, taking a stony little road that dropped steeply to the sea. There was something strange about the place, maybe more than one thing; above all, the large size of the square compared to the few houses that surrounded it. Then I noticed the perfect geometry of the garden with its central fountain, which echoed the shape of the island, then the church that dominated the main square from a height which appeared to be both nearby and far off. I had stopped in a miniscule wine bar where a little old man with shining eyes served wine and fruit liqueurs to the few workmen who were sitting against the wall with their stools tipped back against the wall, a position in perfect harmony with those bodies and which gave an indication of the intolerable heat they must have been feeling as they sat and sweated. I ordered a strawberry liqueur, but the old man shook his head.

With the heat at this time of day you won't be able to breathe properly if you have that, he said. Have something cool. People here are used to drinking whatever the weather, but you are a stranger here and you have to get back in your car. Have a fruit juice.

As he said that, he turned to an old refrigerator with rusty corners, the kind whose handle is broken and will only yield to the touch of the owner who has known it for a long time.

Where are you staying?

At Arcos.

Do you like it? It's very beautiful, but I'd like a change.

Have you been staying there a while? No, just a few days, but...

And as I said it I felt I didn't know what else I would say, but I didn't have much time to think about it because those shining eyes were waiting for an answer. I pulled the tab on my can of Sumol just to hear the noise, which sounded like a rifle shot, a starting gun. I said: It's because of the bathroom, urine soaks through the tiles and it smells bad.

He touched his badly shaven chin, that thin and white hair which gives an opal coloured light to the elderly.

That's bad, he said, when the bathroom's like that you're better off without it. I'm almost eighty and I've never had one... just a shed outside, the old kind, just at the bottom of the stairs, and a tub to wash myself.

I thought of João Freitas. he would have been offended to hear me speaking about his house like that since it had just been done up and you could still smell the fresh paint on the front door.

But there was no going back now. Too often in life there is no time to think. We should be able to say, I need a little time to think before I answer your question, otherwise you tend to find yourself slap in the middle of an effect without a cause. If I'd taken my time I might have been able to tell him the real reason, but now I would have to retrace my steps and that would make a bad impression. I should have said to him: Look, I got a little carried away and I actually made up that story about the bathroom, but it wasn't true at all; I felt time passing slowly and it seemed a torture. But now I can explain to you properly why I want to change house, you see, it's really a very simple matter. When I arrived at Arcos, I saw only João Freitas, he was friendly towards me, and that seemed a very beautiful part of it, together with the fact that the few people who were around all came from the island. But it's not like that at all. In the winter Arcos might well be paradise on earth, but it's the summer now and there are all these emigrants who have come back for the holidays. Don't misunderstand me, I have nothing against them, who does the island belong to if not to them, but they've brought their children with them and they are American, they speak English, they wear huge brightly coloured swimming trunks, they're very fat, and they spend all day hunting poor rabbits which they roast in the evening at one another's houses, smothered with tomato ketchup and they eat calling each other's names loudly even if they're sitting right opposite them at the same table, you see. One of them even uses a megaphone and thinks he's being very clever. But he doesn't speak into it with his normal voice, oh no, he pretends he's an astronaut speaking from outer space and that's how he announces dinner is ready and all the others fall about laughing. I have travelled a very great distance to be away from my own country for a while since people there, too, have taken on too many American ways, and now I find myself slap bang in the middle of these people, and I feel as though I'm going mad, everything's going sour on me. But it was too late now, what I had said was said forever. A spoilt tourist just like all the rest wandering around the world. There was nothing I could do about it.

I finished drinking my Sumol in silence. Before I left, he said, Don't forget to go and see the church, it's our pride and joy, it's an enormous church. He repeated it twice, with the almost angry enthusiasm that always resides in the word enormous. I left the little taverna and began to climb up the slope under the huge and suffocating sun.

There are phrases which wrap themselves up in a moving tenderness: it was just a church, somewhat on the large side. But there are situations where we can put things right, because if I had unwittingly lied to him, now I could ease my conscience by visiting his church. He would never know if I'd been to see it or not, but that was beside the point. It wasn't enormous, but size wasn't that important after all, it was a gloomy church with a melancholy atmosphere and a rough, wooden floor on which my footsteps could be clearly heard. Four elderly women were reciting the rosary kneeling on the altar steps. You couldn't feel lonely in there because of the plethora of statues, all very similar to the one belonging to João Freitas, but twice as high, with clumps of fresh hortensia around their feet. There was something soft about them, they were worn and unreal as toys, they were perched on clouds of gesso that could have been marzipan and they transmitted an idea of simple faith, almost edible, without those thoughts which come along to confuse us. A faith based in the sentimental purity of childhood. Beneath each statue was the name of the Saint, and in the centre of the altar there was the *Ecce Homo* with a long wig down to his shoulders. There was nothing to laugh about, I had learnt that much; he became a man and he, too, had hair.

I don't know how long I stayed in the church, but when I came out again the sun was beating down a little less fiercely and a breeze had got up, which made it possible to breathe a little more freely. As I headed down to the port, I realised that Prainha didn't end here, it continued to the left, ending in a dirt road along the lava coast which went on as far as the lighthouse. That was where I had my first swim, a brief dip at the risk of rheumatism because these waters lead an independent life, never changed by the heat of the sun, but subject, even on the surface, to their vast depths. As I dried off stretched out on the rocks, I could almost feel my damp bones creaking, specially those around my neck. It occurred to me that every illness distorts your vision of things, that water was too cold only for me; anybody else could go in and out as they pleased, like that little boy who had been levering *lapas* off the rocks with a penknife for more than an hour. And when he got old, would he still be levering off *lapas,* only touched by other ills and other fears, I thought, watching him hard at work crouched over the rock like a spider.

A sudden strange fear of death swept over me, a small pain between my ribs began to press against my heart, or perhaps it was just an idea that had sent a shiver over my skin, dry now in the sun. I started up and wanted to look all around me to make sure that everything still had the same outlines. But lying with your eyes closed under the sun has a strange effect when you open them again, you should never choose that moment to look for the real outlines of the world. With this uneasiness in me, I set off back along the dirt road which led to the lighthouse, kept company by the houses in lava stone which lay along it, oscillating in the sun.

A man about sixty years old was coming down with slow steps, the sun behind his back. I was struck by the huge mass of his hair lit by the sunlight, and the faded trousers, which left his thin ankles bare. He walked bent over by a hump which rose up on his left shoulder like a small mountain, and he held his neck in the position of a vegetarian animal, stretched slightly down towards the earth, in a soft curve. For him, the road was going down, so at first I saw him against the sky, then almost attached to the shadow of the earth. As he passed me, he slowed his pace even more and gave me a kindly smile. It was certainly owing to his gentle manner that once more, for the second time that day, I hurried to speak before thinking. Just to smile back at him didn't seem enough to me, and so, even though I had never met him before, I asked him:

Excuse me, you wouldn't happen to know if anyone has a house to rent around here? He rested his chin on the bony fingers of his right hand, almost an inverted tripod to support that thin head. He stood there collecting his thoughts, looking at the depths of the road. Then he let go his hold, letting his chin wobble slightly. If I remember rightly, it might well be this one right here, he said, pointing to the house in front of us. It belongs to signor João Antonio, who works at the *Banca Comercial* in Cais do Pico, and so saying he pushed with his hand at the wooden garden gate.

It's closed of course, he said, but if you go in through here you can see the garden at least, go up the outside steps and take in the view.

He was still pushing, and said there must be a latch closed on the inside. Then, without adding a word, he made himself very thin, his hump disappeared too and he squeezed through the opening, passing through to the other side. Now I can open it for you, he said. Yes, it was the latch.

We found ourselves in a garden with no plants in it, in undulating lava stone, left just as the ancient flows from the volcano had made it. You must go up the steps, he said, looking at me from the terrace. From here you can see the whole coast. I just had to go up a few steps and up there was another climate, much windier, and a view that was absolutely stunning. We stood there for a moment in silence, the man with his arms folded, his worn out, faded cotton shirt sticking to the skinniness of his ribs which rippled like the lava rock. He looked out at the sea with a profile so bony that he seemed transparent, offering no obstacle to the wind.

Everyone gets used to what they see, he said, without looking at me, and in the end he can't imagine anything more beautiful. My house is on this same road, a little further on, towards the port.

He says that like someone who has never been away, I thought, still silent, but he turned to me as if I had spoken without realizing it.

You are wrong, he said. Almost twenty years in Canada breathing in cloth dye. It was a mistake to go, all I got over there was a terrible illness. But you are well now, aren't you? I asked. Oh yes, certainly. Life is simple; you get sick only to get better again.

He went down the steps first and looked up at me from below. This really is a lovely place; I hope João Antonio hasn't come to some agreement with some other foreigner. Go straight away, tomorrow, to the *Banca Comercial*, you'll see, he's a very nice young man is signor João Antonio. Tell him that Julio Neves has sent you.

We walked along the road together while the sun, behind our backs, started the long slow descent of the sunset. You could see it from the long thin shadows of our bodies, which the earth seemed to soak up like water. After a bit I stopped him. What about this one, I asked him, would you know if this house is available for rent too? This is the house of signor Aurelio, he answered me.

It looks uninhabited, I said.

He lives somewhere else now, that's why.

Emigrated?

No, still here.

I can talk to him then.

That would be difficult.

Where does he live now?

Over there, said Julio Neves, making a vague gesture with his right hand.

Can we see it from where we are now?

No, not from here, he replied. From here, it's a long way.

I realised that insisting would get me nowhere, so I said to him: Well, thank you so much, and I went to shake his hand.

If you are not in a hurry I could show you my house, said Julio Neves, it's just next door to signor Aurelio's house.

Where I come from, we don't usually accept invitations from strangers, but here it's different, a world without mistrust, where thoughts expressed with words hold nothing hidden behind them.

The house of Julio Neves seemed the most abandoned of them all. I was taken aback by a pair of old trousers hanging up to dry which could have been there for years, left there to go stiff as a board with the sun and rain of heavens knows how many seasons. We stayed in the garden, and for this I have no other explanation than the custom of times gone by that a man and a woman should never be under the same roof together unless they are connected by some family bond. He offered me some wine which had a strange flavour. Any other time I would have said it had gone off, but at that moment it just seemed to me to be very old wine.

He had no family, Julio Neves, he had never been a married man in that shadowy house. I looked at his skinny chest and thought it was from here that he breathed his few words, and then I looked at his head, which must have been heavy on his thin neck. He sipped his wine slowly, it was *vinho de cheiro* like all the wine on the island, pressed from the minute black grape which covers the lower slopes of the hills and is surrounded by little dry stone walls or bushes of hortensia. I felt as if we had much to say to each other, as happens between silent people, but we remained absorbed within our own thoughts and all I said to him was that it was getting late and I had to go. As we said goodbye, the sun had gone down into the sea and the sky had turned the beautiful violent colours of the Azores, those colours which fill the soul with a kind of euphoria for who knows what unknown future, and at the same time full of regret for the many things we have not done in our life and which we cannot even remember. Fearing that I would forget his name, he wanted to tell me it again.

Don't forget to say to signor João Antonio that you have come on my recommendation, Julio Neves.

And I nodded as I turned back up to the little taverna where I had left my rented car.

❦

I awoke early the next morning and did as Julio Neves had advised. The *Banca Comercial* in Cais do Pico was a small room divided down the middle by a wooden screen. On this side, the side which could be seen, a single employee sat behind a counter. As she filled in her index cards by hand, it was hard to tell what age she was. As she watched me come in, she let her glasses slip down to the end of her nose and at the same time her lower lip fell in expressive harmony, becoming humid and round.

Can I help you? she asked.

I would like to know if signor João Antonio works here.

He certainly does, he's the director of this bank.

I need to speak to him, I said.

The woman came down off her stool and walked away, an obvious defect in her hip making her walk slowly. She disappeared behind the screen and I could hear only her voice.

Sir, there's a foreign lady who would like to speak to you.

Tell her to come in, Adelaide.

The woman came back and lifted up a corner of the counter to let me through.

Please come in, the Director will see you straight away.

Had I followed my instinct, I should have said, I'm so sorry, there must be some mistake. But sometimes instinct plays strange tricks on us when it is overwhelmed by surprise. I'd expected a young man and instead the man in front of me must have been at least fifty years old, he was several kilos overweight and had a bored expression in his face, which gave little impression of kindness or gentleness. This time, too, I spoke because I had no time to think of anything else. I couldn't stand in silence any length of time in front of this man who just looked at me, without putting me at my ease. The words came tumbling out as I was still on my feet, just the tips of my fingers resting on his desk and leaning forward very slightly.

Are you the owner of the house at Prainha?

His eyebrows shot up, together with the shiny skin of his forehead and I said to myself, there, he looks a little younger now, without considering that the reason for this sudden change was nothing other than astonishment at my question which was so direct and so imprecise at the same time.

He even started to laugh.

Yes Madame, I have a house at Prainha, one of the many that you can find there.

He gave me his hand, slightly puffy with the heat, and with the other he invited me to sit down.

I am sorry, I said, I didn't express myself very well; I know only a few words and almost no verbs. I understand pretty well, but speaking is another matter altogether. He crossed his hands over his stomach and arched his back slightly—a man accustomed to listening to other peoples requests.

Well, he said again, smiling, first of all let me try to understand if we are talking about the same house, mine is the one along the row of cliffs which starts down at the port, roughly half way between the port and the lighthouse.

That's the one, I answered, I wanted to know if it is still free, because if it is, I would like to rent it for a couple of months.

He unfolded his hands, which were covered in black hair, and placed them on the desk.

I haven't rented it out for years, many years, since my son went away to work in the United States. He comes back every year now, with his family, they spend a month here, sometimes less, then they go back over there until another year comes round. But even before that I didn't let it out very often; there have never been many tourists round these parts.

I understand, I'm sorry to have troubled you, I said.

How did you find me? he asked. And once more I realised that I had misjudged time, using it wrongly and leaving to the end what I should have said right at the start. I was leaving now, already on my feet. Julio Neves sent me, I said, and I saw those eyebrows of his return to their natural position and I saw his forehead settle back into the creases of old age.

That must mean that on the contrary, you speak better than you understand, he said, looking straight into my eyes. It's not uncommon, they pronounce names so fast around here that it's difficult for a foreigner to understand them properly, you must have mistaken one for another. I don't remember the exact date now, but Julio Neves died over twenty years ago. He went to Canada and contracted some horrible disease, he came back here to Pico just to die. It happens to many of them when they leave to do menial jobs, they don't come back until it's too late. I'm sorry I cannot rent you my house, but you will find any number of them. There are fewer and fewer people around here.

I left the *Banca Comercial* accompanied by the irregular footsteps of the lady called Adelaide. Outside the sky had been cleared of clouds by the wind and the breeze was stiff, every breath almost suffocating with the waves of air rushing into the lungs.

I went back to Arcos, to the house of João Freitas. I waited for the day to end so I could go to sleep. I fell asleep very quickly, protected by an unnatural absence of thoughts and I don't know when the dream began, but I think it must have been towards dawn, which is when we have our most meaningful dreams. I was walking up the road at Prainha but it was night, with just a weak light coming from the few ancient lampposts. I saw Julio Neves coming down as I had seen him in real life, but illuminated by the blue reflections of the lighthouse, which washed over him in the colours of the other world. When he was close to me, I said to him: I've come back this way because I was really hoping to see you. I need to ask you something very important. He turned to me with his eyes half closed, like someone struggling to remember something. He asked: Do you know me? Of course, don't you remember? I asked you if there was a house to let and you pointed me to the house of João Antonio. He had a strange expression on his face, a smile perhaps. I've lost my memory, he said softly. Lost it completely, I can only remember things from way back. At that time of night he couldn't do anything else except turn back towards his house, and so I walked with him for a while as the sea slipped among the lava rocks almost without a sound. He seemed to me to be talking to himself, but perhaps it was just his thoughts, something confused which had to do with who knows what torment. I said to him, You know, signor João Antonio told me you died over twenty years ago, but I don't believe him because you and I met and we spoke together, we even drank a glass of wine. The dead don't do these things. But then there's the story of the *Bom Jesus Milagroso* and João Freitas' wife, who even though she was dead walked and talked as if she were still alive. I haven't been here very long and if this is just the start...

He stopped suddenly and something like a shudder ran through him. What did signor João Antonio tell you? He said that you were dead. Are you absolutely sure? That's what he said. Then it must be true, he said with a heavy sigh. It's just that I don't remember anything, but if that's what he said it must be true, and that must be why I feel a great emptiness and I never know anything. Now you're taking as gospel what could be nothing more than a misunderstanding, I said to him. Maybe you're just tired, maybe it's something left over from that illness you had. Signor João Antonio must have got you muddled up with someone else, because believe me, I'm no expert but everybody knows that the dead are always the first to realise that they are dead. He looked at me as if I had said something very unconvincing.

Signor Neves, did you understand what I said to you?

I know what you said, but it's not true at all.

∗

When I awoke, my heart was at peace and I felt fine. But I had no choice; I had to go back to Prainha and visit the cemetery.

It wasn't difficult to find, it was on a little mound and from there you could see the sea whichever way you turned. The sadness of cemeteries is a very relative thing. This one had a strange effect on me, almost playful. But perhaps that was because it was so small, so carefully kept, and a multitude of fresh flowers shone in the sun from every tomb. It was divided into two parts by a long path. At the back, placed on the ground so that from a distance it looked like a throne, was the funeral cart, still in use today. There was nothing macabre about it, indeed it was the same shape and colour of rural artefacts from other times. Even when one looked at it carefully, it was difficult to imagine a dead body on it—what came to mind were two oxen tied to the cart and pulling it over a lovely field.

The tomb of Julio Neves was one of the last ones. In relief, on the white marble, were the dates of his birth and death:

NASCIDO 23.10.1910

FALECEU 01.02.1975

There was a portrait of him too, but whoever had chosen it wanted to remember him as a young man, because with the man I had met there was only that faintest of similarities which so saddens the old when they look at an image of their past. He had a good head of black hair and a fine moustache that was so thick that it covered his smile. But you could see from his eyes that he was smiling, a sensual smile which could only have been for a woman. You were a very handsome man, I said to him aloud. It was only my imagination, but I felt as if I was being looked at by real eyes, but this often happens with photos of the dead, they take life from our life.

If I'd known his surname, I would have liked to look for the tomb of the mysterious signor Aurelio because I had no doubts now, if he had gone to live so far off as Julio Neves had said, he could only be there amongst all those who had passed on. Before I left the cemetery, I turned back to take a last look at it, so beautiful there in the full sunlight of a perfect clear day, and those bright flowers. You've all chosen a delightful place, I thought. You've been lucky.

When I went back to the house of João Freitas I decided not to look for another one, I was fine there even if there were all those emigrants' sons who spoke American. I was tired, and I went into the bathroom to get off all that reddish dust from my walk along the road from Cachorro to Cabrito. It was just then that I noticed the strong and bitter smell of urine, and to my astonishment I realised that it really was seeping through the floor.

It doesn't matter, I thought. It's my own body fluid, I'll wash it every day. I wouldn't have dreamt of telling João Freitas, he would have been like a cat on a hot tin roof until he had found out where the fault was.

In the damp drops on the white tiles I thought I saw once more the luke-warm gaze of Julio Neves, a gaze in which irony and sensuality intermingled. Around here they call it *olhar trocista*.

Chapter four

Maria Moniz

From where I am, sitting under the porch, I can see her walking on the lava stone in a way that is almost unreal, because no woman of her age could walk so lightly, not even a young woman. Seen like that it is a miracle, as if she were walking on water. It's a vision that is romantic and grotesque at the same time, because the woman dressed in mourning, who steps forward with the aid of a stick, always makes the same brief journey which takes her to a small cement outhouse, a cube-like block, where she retires to relieve herself.

From where I am looking, I can see three of these cement constructions, and if a line were to be drawn between them, they would form a harmonious semicircle held together by the blue of the sea. The one which belongs to the woman is the last, the one closest to the cliff, and so when she passes by she really does seem as if suspended, a childish drawing, infantile and sophisticated at the same time.

She probably doesn't realise it, but every time she make this journey the woman carries out a ritual. I should say straight off that she appears as if from nowhere, because between her house and mine there is another, the one on my left. And so her appearance always has something theatrical and mysterious about it: the fusion of her sombre-coloured mourning clothes and the brightness of the sky. To my eyes she is melancholy incarnate, and she conveys a loss born from something deep inside her that transforms itself into a contagious regret in whoever happens to be watching her. She's a heavy woman, deformed by old age, her legs swollen from poor circulation. You can see this even from a distance because she wears elastic stockings and because her gait is slow and shambling, like the movement of a metallic ship when the sea is calm.

From where I first see her, she can't go much more than twenty or thirty metres as far as the cement outhouse. The first image is of her black dress flapping in the wind. She doesn't move, she contemplates the path like an exhausted pachyderm, lingering on the threshold of my vision, supported by a stick of light-coloured wood. It's as if she were waiting for her strength to return, as if she were concentrating all her energy after some great effort. Just a few moments, but always the same. Then she starts off with that unreal walk of hers, that sliding along, and half way there she stops, turns, and looks at the sea. Perhaps she is catching her breath, or perhaps her legs hurt her, and she is looking at the sea without even seeing it, just to pass the time. When she arrives at her destination, she leaves her stick leaning against the brief expanse of cement wall, opens a small door of rough-hewn wood and, stepping into the dark entrance, shuts it behind her. She is never inside for very long, she is a healthy woman who only undertakes that journey to the outhouse when she has a real need, but she must be able to control it too, for I never see her hurrying or indeed loitering in the manner of someone who is just going to try. She comes out and goes through the whole ritual in reverse, and, just as on the way out, she stops half way to look out at the sea.

There are some things which last for long periods of time, others which on the other hand are instantly consumed. Sometimes we feel the need to go beyond a gesture and meet face to face with the person who makes it, even at the risk of disappointment.

It was for this reason that I waited only a few days before going to take a closer look. The first time I did it in secret, towards sunset, when the woman was still inside her house. I wanted to see that journey she made, and make it myself, keeping scrupulously to the same lengths of time that I had observed from a distance. Even that might have been an immediate disappointment, but when we set off in search of revelations we have to do it with an open heart. And so I discovered that if despite her age she walked so gently and softly over the rocks it was because the loving thoughtfulness and affection, of a son perhaps, had smoothed them down for her with goodness knows how much effort of muscle and sweat, tracing out a path for her which he had then sprinkled over with the finest gravel.

I took the same steps as she did, I arrived as far as the point where she stopped to look out at the sea, where the ground was most worn away, in a faded circle. In front of the cement outhouse I felt, as she must, that I, too, had covered a great distance, I too felt the same weariness over my whole body, the same old age and the same fear of death. And then I wondered what on earth could be the meaning of this I too, and how I could express it. I certainly had no idea what would be going through her mind after that pilgrimage. You're identifying too much with everything around you, I thought, lighten up a little, this is just an old habit of yours—swallowing up the person next to you.

But I'd done it now—no sooner said than done—the thought as good as a deed from which there is no escape. And so I opened that tiny door after miming the setting aside of a walking stick, and I tried to be her, inside there in the darkness of stale smell which was aired only by a minute window, held half closed by an iron-coloured lava stone. Through a slit in the wall you could see the sky and the sea, the solitary and single-coloured point of contact with the out-side world. Inside, there was a plank, damp with brine and a circular hole as precise as if it had been drawn with a compass. It might seem lacking in poetry to say that this was where she put her rear end but this is a lack of poetry in the language because the idea, as opposed to the act itself, remains of a celestial purity.

Outside, even the light of the sunset was dazzling. Once again the same journey back, step by step, stopping half way along to look at the sea, which was crossed only by a far off ship faint in the mist. On the way back home, I thought how different distances were, my steps were certainly slower than the ship and yet I seemed to leave it far behind as I was walking. In the lingering brightness of the sky, the stars were beginning to come out.

The next day I asked João Freitas who the woman was. My aunt, he said. She just spends the summers here, in the winter she stays in Santa Luzia. She's here on her own; once a week the son of one of her cousins does some shopping for her. If you would like to go and see her she would be very happy, she loves company, in her own way.

I went the next day, in the early hours of an afternoon filled with sun and wind. I found her sitting in the shade, in front of her house, on a narrow bench that she had placed right up against the wall. I went up to her and said that I had been living for a few days in the house of her nephew João Freitas and that I was there to pay her a visit, if she would like that. She welcomed me with a lovely movement of her head, that way of tilting it backwards and then bringing it forward again very slowly. I couldn't think of anything else to say to her, and this time I decided to follow my instinct since it was usually sound, the one that whispered to me not to look for any more words. Taking that gesture of hers for an invitation, I sat down next to her and flattened my back against the wall. I would love to have been able to observe her now that I was so close to her, but some things can be taken for rudeness, you can run the risk of offending someone even when that is not your intention. From where I was sitting I could look out to sea and the almost endless cliffs which fell down so sharply in places that they seemed to take the shape of animals, but rather than that, since I could not look at her, I looked at that extension of her, the cement outhouse illuminated by a light so strong it seemed to make it all the more long and narrow.

Sometimes it is easier than we think to express a thought, especially if it is apparently bizarre and somewhat senseless. It came out with the utmost spontaneity because it was completely genuine. And so I broke a silence that had lasted I don't know how long and said to her: Don't ask me why, but I have the impression that I am you.

She sat calm and still, she didn't even turn towards me, she stayed looking out, and since I had been the one to speak, I felt justified in looking at her at least for a moment. She was extraordinarily compact, head, body and legs formed three strangely identical blocks of astonishing harmony, three helmets with a lowered visor arranged as a human body. The same was true of her head, and difficult as it might be to imagine the trunk of a body and a pair of legs as a helmet, that's the way it appeared, and in the bright sunlight of the day they glowed with an almost golden light. The three main points were the nose, the breast and the knees, they were the absolutely central point of each helmet, the nose which descended parallel to her entire face, stopping only shortly before its end, in a clear line, just like her breast in relation to her body and her legs in relation to her generous hips. Three helmets which took on the shape of a woman and also the throne on which she was seated.

I was thinking this when she answered: We are all a bit the same person.

Then she went back to being silent, completely absorbed, intact, enclosed within a single thought that must have occupied her entire being. Who knows what she meant, here they are all so religious that they go so far as to pray on the church steps when the church is closed, their foreheads resting against the locked door. Perhaps being a bit the same person meant belonging to the divine totality which governs the world, or perhaps it was a different thought, nothing to do with belief, which far from enriching the world, actually impoverishes it.

Then she got up slowly, helping herself with her stick, and dragging herself on those swollen legs she went into the house and signalled me to follow her.

The rite she carried out was no longer new to me. She did the same as João Freitas, washing and rewashing a flowery glass in the water that she poured out in a steady stream from an upturned basin. And when she poured me something to drink from an unmarked bottle, I had no need to ask her what it was, because around here it's always homemade *angelica*. I drank alone as she watched me, and I realised without being told that from that moment we were becoming to each other, because the woman sat at the dining table, spread her hands on a waxed cloth stripped of any colour by the years, and looked me in the eyes. Now that I had her properly in front of me she seemed to me rather beautiful in her old age, almost majestic.

Your nephew told me you're alone here, I said to her.

My husband died twelve years ago.

What about your children?

In America. They come here sometimes, and they write me letters. I can't read, you know, I hear what they write when the postman reads their letters to me.

Do you ever go to see them there?

I can't travel with these legs. I've even had two veins taken out, but that didn't make much of a difference. I can't walk very well.

They all go off to America, I said. There will be nobody left here.

It's very sad, she answered me.

She turned to look at the open door, drawn by the beauty of the light. She stood up and went to sit back outside, on the bench, with her back against the wall of the house. It's hot today, she said, waving her hand in front of her face. It's the humidity. And having uttered these words all she left me to see was her profile drawn against the dark blue of a sky that had taken on the colour of the sea.

Perhaps I really could have been that woman, but who knows in what other time, and whether it had been in the past or was still to come. I, too, leaned back against the wall of the house and I don't know how long we sat there, because at one point I think I must have closed my eyes in a torpor that seemed to have no start or end.

I left when the sun was still high, but this doesn't mean a thing because there can be entire days without nights and many nights without days when thought is suspended, days of just day and nights of just night; a continual return of the same waitfulness.

I didn't know how to say goodbye to her. I could go off quietly; perhaps she wouldn't even notice I had gone. But such a discretion might have been misunderstood and so, as I tend to do when I feel I am running out of time, I said something stupid to her.

Don't you get bored sitting here all the time looking at the sea?

No.

What do you think about?

I think about my life.

Now as I see her walking slowly, I know exactly the ground signora Maria Moniz is treading, and I know she is not unreal. Sometimes, half way, when she stops to look at the ocean and breathe in the wind, she turns in my direction. Perhaps she can't always manage to see me against the sun and at that distance, but if she thinks I might be there watching her, she waves with her hand, and I do the same.

Chapter five

Malvina Sebastião

Do you know what I used to do when I was young? I used to dance the *chamarrita*. I would happily show you what it's like—but now the bones up and down my back ache, and that's a dance where you really shake yourself about. I can show you the arm movements that are like this, and then you do this, but you can't really get an idea of the whole thing from that. It's not an easy dance, you know. You have to work hard at it because it's made up of many different patterns and you need someone in the group to have a strong voice to call out when to close and open up the circle. Generally it's a man's voice, but when I was young and we used to dance after the fiesta of the *toro*, the bull, often that powerful voice was mine.

She stopped to look at me and then she broke out into a peal of laughter that transformed her into a rare beauty, seductive and bright like a serpent. And so I thought she might have been born of the union between a South American with a beautiful serpent of the *sertao*, the ones that have joyful names like Yarananà and deliver either ecstasy or death with a single bite.

The best thing about Malvina Sebastião is her eyes, and then there's her almost masculine laughter and the absence of age. Prodigious elements, these, which render her human and beast-like at the same time, close to the divinity when it is in pagan form. That day I was listening to her talk about her life as a young woman, while she stirred a pan where she was boiling twelve kilos of blackberries which she had picked the same morning somewhere near Figueira. She was warming herself at her improvised fire out in the open, in front of her house, and she was getting covered with the damp smoke, almost as if it was real sweat.

She had to prepare her blackberry liqueur well ahead of time, at least a year before her son arrived from Canada, and this time she wanted to make it really good, of the kind that ages well in bottles in the cool of the cellar.

Malvina Sebastião makes you feel safe; she seems happy. Just as for all those who have been on the face of this earth a very long time, this can't have been true at all, but the thing that struck you about her, the wonderful thing about her, lies precisely in this appearance which takes you in when you look at her, and not just for the first time. She has the ability to keep life at a distance through an absolute and total participation in life itself. This might seem a contradiction, but in this way she really does keep it at arm's length and never abandons herself to sorrow. As I watch her, I think that hers is wisdom without origin, entirely circular, and that she has fallen into the middle of it.

Do you know what my mother used to say, she asks, pulling a wooden spoon stained bloody with cooked blackberries out of the mixture. She used to say that passions are for … I won't say it, it's a bad word, and my mother was an unhappy woman, because life without passions would drive you mad. Do you know what she used to do? She was always thinking, and that's not much good for you, it makes you feel empty and sad. In life, you shouldn't let your thoughts go with you, you should go with them, and sometimes send them on their own way, which is not necessarily the same path as ours. Do you know how old I am? Sixty-five, sixty-five years, all of them mine. There are not many who can say that. Two half-naked little boys, her grandchildren, buzz around her, coloured red all over with the dark blackberry juice, their tongues almost blue by now. The smallest one is crying because he's been bitten by an ant, which was crawling around the fruit. It bit my tongue, he says, grizzling. That's because you chat on too much, she consoles him, holding all his hair in one hand. And then she laughs, covered in sweat, her narrow eyes like melon seeds criss-crossed by a thousand black lights. Her teeth are tiny, you only see them when she opens her mouth to laugh, never when she speaks. She clicks her fingers, still raising her arms in the movement of the *chamarrita*, but without minding me, perhaps just to cheer up her grandson, who is still crying. The older child eats a boiled corn on the cob sitting on the steps of the house, while he is hitting the lava rock with a piece of iron, staring straight in front of him. He seems to be doing it just to hear the noise.

Now I'm fine, Malvina Sebastião tells me, my life is peaceful and calm. People should appreciate life, yet instead everybody spouts a heap of nonsense about sorrow. Do you believe that life is one big sorrow? I don't believe it. Too many days each the same as the next, so much the same that you don't even notice it. It's work, that's what life is above all. People are afraid of forgetting, but I try telling people to stay in the present, maybe a bit unaware of anything else, what do you think? I waited patiently all the time I was over there in Canada. Eighteen years, not just a few days. I had a husband and three children, in the end I understood American, but I never learnt to speak it. I didn't suffer, but I never fully adapted either. I always found that astonishing in other people. At the beginning I had to console them, help them find the good things about the place we were all in, then, as the months and the years began to roll by, I had to start backtracking and do the opposite. Hang out the sheets together with the other women and say: But have you all forgotten our own land?

I had to cross the street holding the children by the hand and turn round to my sister-in-law who was coming behind me doing the same, and say: It's a fiesta in Pico today, another month and the heavy rains will start. Just the thought of that might send a shudder through her, and I would push the point. They were wonderful, those heavy rains of ours, those were the best. That's how for some people coming back was as bad as going; they found themselves rootless all over again. Maybe that's why they come away with that business about life being one long sorrow; because they are stuck in the past and over there they are looking to the future.

Twice she tasted that thick, burning liquid after blowing on it silently, just to try it for flavour. Then she began mixing again.

Do you like to laugh? she asked. It's a great satisfaction, a way of feeling feverish even when you are in perfectly good health. Everyone has a special laughter place, I can feel it running down my arm here, running down inside, like happy blood which goes skipping off by itself. Everybody has their bad moments, but it's much better if they keep them to themselves, because if you go around going on about it you risk infecting everyone else. I was quite content over there, I didn't like it but I was content, and I let the days go by without counting them, and forgetting them when night fell. I did what I could to stay in one piece; it's no easy feat. I knew that I had to be on top of things, my gestures. I don't know if I'm explaining myself, getting dinner ready and being that dinner, cleaning the window and being that moving arm, that clean window. The others suffered and then forgot, but I was the things themselves. Would you like to try it?

She lifted the steaming wooden spoon to my lips and we blew on it together, because the more the liquid caramelised over the fire the more likely it was to burn.

If you want to take a drop back to your own country you can buy it here, everybody makes it, but here in Pico, if you buy it at São Miguel, it's more syrup than liqueur. My husband worked in the building trade, a simple labourer. Now that I think about it, there was an Italian engineer over there for a while, my husband learnt to say a few words in Italian, he liked it, and that engineer was a really nice gentleman. Some get by well in life and others have a much harder time. My husband was one of those who had no luck at all, but he never complained, he lived and died with dignity. But let's not talk about death now, it will just make us sad, you end up getting too close to it, you end up being death itself, and that's dangerous. I have always thought that I wouldn't like to go backwards and I wouldn't like to go forwards, I just want to be exactly in the moment where I am, the one magnificent moment of uncertainty. When I wake up I never understand that I am alive—does that ever happen to you? So I start to move my hands and feet slowly, because that's where life is, and that always puts me in a good mood. I know that I have a day of work ahead of me. Over there, in Canada, the winter cold used to frighten me, so many other things used to frighten me, including the way I just wanted not to say anything. When you change your world there is something that just falls silent; if it's out of surprise it doesn't last long, if it's out of fear you have to find your speech again quickly. I wanted to find the good things about those years, the unexpectedly good things. Do you know what it is? Maybe this is just my own invention, I've already mentioned it to you, it's the way I have of letting things flow without following them too closely, going with them without letting them go with you. I think I have saved much of my life, and now I can pick the good fruits of old age without the other things that normally afflict the old. Now watch.

As she said that, she took the pan off the flames and started to pour off the liquid, leaving the fruit on the bottom. By now the fruit had turned into a mush. She did it slowly, and very ably.

Now whatever's left of the blackberries is fit to be thrown away, she said, it's no good any more. It's like our bodies when the moment of death finally arrives, the substance goes off elsewhere and doesn't want to be weighed down. This is the great danger of life, the sorrow that we no longer want to abandon. I learnt that lesson watching a lot of other people. Sometimes it seems as though all people do is become expert in sorrow, their own sorrow. And to begin with, it hurts like an open wound when you rub salt into it, then, with time, you don't seem to feel it any more but it isn't true, it's that you've been overwhelmed by it and you don't notice because you have no healthy spaces left, you've become one with your pain. This is a terrible danger because, with the passing of time, the bad thing goes right to the bottom, into the depths of your being, and feeds it, makes it heavy, and when the soul is on the point of taking its leave, it's confused, it doesn't know how to take the light road of height which it should rightly go on and it stays here, on earth, it stays here even though it knows this is no longer its proper place. Now, if I tell you that there are any number of these ghostly beings amongst the living, you'll think I'm mad. But I'm telling you that I can feel them, I can feel them as if I could see them with a special inner eye of mine, and when I meet them it grieves me for there is nothing I can do, because the living have no power over these things, they stay alive, do you see what I mean? This island is full of them, as you'll see for yourself. That house down there, for example, the one at the end of the road that they call the priest's house, even though the priest never comes here because he's in America, well, in front of that house, in the garden, there's a strange plant with a single large flower which hasn't faded for years, which always looks fresh and new. Sometimes, at night, exactly where the plant is, there's a man from another time, a plant-man who comes back because of the need to show himself to whoever can and wants to see him. But nobody can go near him, just look from a distance, that's all. He seems to count every step of mine every time I go anywhere near him to take a closer look, no more than five and then he disappears. I know it is a soul, one of the many that I see—a soul that, in his time, has lived too much within the sorrow of the world. We should understand before it's too late that this is no joking matter and pray to God to absolve us all.

Do you know what I think? Exactly the opposite of what we normally think, I think we haven't come into the world to suffer. The God of the universe is too good to want harm for us poor creatures of the earth. All this about suffering is the work of the devil, stuff which is put into our head by the one who has as much power as the Lord God of the universe, and who shares this kingdom with him. It's a facile belief to think that suffering strengthens us, but that's not why we were created and put on the face of the earth. When I say things like this people take me for a heretical witch, and that's strange, don't you think? But life is a gift made for joy, and suffering, when it arrives, is only something which we should let accompany us at a distance of several paces, and we should say to it, don't follow me, go another way and let me see the back of you. As strange as it might seem to you, I think life is easy to go along with, naturally divided into different phases. The secret is not to desire anything of the past or the future, and to look with the gentleness of our feelings on all things, whether it's the joy of birth or the sadness of death, as things that will not last. Now I've said enough and the liqueur is ready. All I have to do now is add the alcohol and bottle it for my son. I'll not add anything to what I've said, just that I believe I have lived well, here in my old age and over there in Canada as a young woman, when I danced the *chamarrita* to remind myself of the place where I was born, but without suffering, with pleasure... you make this movement with your arms ... and then this one, without feeling any pain in the bones of your back.

Chapter six
Drink

In life few things give as much relief as discovering that a horrible man is not so horrible as we thought. It is not a question of absolving our neighbour, but of absolving ourselves for judging badly and too hastily. It's a matter of our conscience and our conscience, as we know, speaks its own silent language, which works slowly but as powerfully as a highly corrosive acid.

About that time I had noticed João Freitas coming and going around a house which up till now had been shut up in silent abandonment, a big house, on the other side of the red road, the only one in Arcos with a proper fence around it. I didn't want to think about it, I watched him coming and going, opening the windows, standing on the veranda for a while, having a smoke while the air dried up all the damp which had created its own smells inside the house. It's just his way, I said to myself, he likes to keep things in order even when they don't belong to him. But then I saw him pulling up the shutters of a garage and pushing out, by sheer force of effort, a car that belonged almost to a bygone age. I said to him: You're not hoping to get that going, are you? And he raised his eyes to where I was looking out of the window and fanned himself with his *Azores Concrete* cap. Certainly I'm going to get it going, he answered me. It's a great old banger, and the owner's arriving tomorrow.

I went back into the house and shut the window. More Americans, I thought, there'll be no peace around here, and I spent what remained of the day walking along the cliffs where all you could see was the great ocean, the swelling up of huge lengths of wave, the roar as they crashed against the black rock because seeing and hearing, in solitude, are one and the same thing.

❦

The next day João Freitas went to get the Americans himself, in the old banger, which, considering its age, wasn't in fact too noisy. It's just a short trip from Arcos to the airport, just a few minutes, and so João Freitas had gone and come back in the time it took me to say to myself, soon there will be another house opened up, clothes hanging out, chairs on the veranda, who knows how much noise and how many new voices. I don't know how long I went on repeating this fear of mine to myself. I know that I only stopped when I saw them arrive, and heaved a sigh of relief when I counted just two people apart from João Freitas himself. A decrepit-looking couple got out of the car and wearily started unloading an impressive amount of luggage. This shifting of a whole life was rather a melancholy sight, and more touching than anything was the fact that this was almost certainly not a real removal but just a summer dislocation, the same as for everybody else, after goodness only knows how much time away. It must have been a long time indeed since they had been here if they needed to set up everything around them like this, drinking it in themselves and showing it to anyone who might be watching them as they unloaded an entire house. A catastrophic return, as their departure must have been, taking with them every last single thing. This is what you see in the cinema, I thought to myself, I wonder how many films start just like this. I stayed at the window looking at all this human movement. By now I knew full well how these things turned out—the first few days the great dance around their new life, then visits to all the other houses, welcome back parties, talking and talking at the tops of their voices, struggling to express every single thing that passes through their heads. In the evening, there are the people you meet in the street, everybody sitting in a circle around the well, in the faint light thrown off by the lamps, a weak light which gives the night a shiny hue, and people's faces softened by the darkness of night.

At these times there was indeed consolation to be found in words, everyone with his thoughts all ready for the off-with-that habit they have of never enjoying things as they are, and that intermingling of Portuguese and American when they say 'it's OK' even over here, so far away from the place where supermarkets are open twenty four hours a day and the streets always lit, and all the rest. But after a bit they say little, by now they've said to each other everything that was ready in their thoughts to be said, now it's just a question of the odd sentence amidst the loud sound of the waves battering violently against the rocks. The big waves are just behind us, yet we seem to be listening to the ones travelling from Cabrito, not from Arcos. And this makes them smile in the emptiness; this still astonishes them, this acoustic quirk of the sea when it has the wind blowing over it.

I know without anyone telling me the way things will turn out, every day a bit less euphoric, a bit more mute, and for this very reason a little more engulfing. I spend my days on the veranda; I've brought a lot of books with me from Italy. I look up towards this house, which has only just been opened up and say to myself: This is no longer just a house, it is their house, with *their* speech, *their* bodies, all *their* weight and heaviness. By now I have developed the vice of seeing the human body as something that ruins any panoramic view, an element that disrupts the aesthetics of each and every place. There are very few who manage to avoid this, and there is one simple rule—being in harmony, a total harmony between person and place. João Freitas is as one with Arcos but his son is not, his son is a grating false note.

The next day this new couple had lunch on the veranda and they must have been eating very slowly because to me it seemed to go on forever. They were eating in the shade of the portico and the day was very sunny and clear, with little wind, and in the sky the flight of the seagulls seemed unmoving, a single line which moved with the slow pace of a distant ship on the horizon. I couldn't help looking at them, and so the woman waved her hand to me and the man, turning round, did the same.

Do you want a little drink?

He shouted over to me smiling strangely, and I shook my head, and said, no thanks, but I must have said it too quietly and against the breeze for them to be able to hear me.

There are things which come back to us, things seen from afar which come back close to us, almost out of proportion because they have suddenly become so large. This is what happened to me with the face of that man which seemed to have separated itself from his body and floated towards me, swollen and red as I had seen it in his smile. I saw it wherever I went and I could hear it speaking too, a kind of drowned man's head, which said: A little drink?

These things, which come back to us and haunt us, become strangely obsessive, they seem to be there just to fill us with fear, and they often succeed in doing just that. They are the opposite of essence, they dilute to the point of multiplying, and so I had the impression that this face was always there just in front of my own, so close that I could only just make out a few huge details: an enormous nose, an enormous stretch of pock-marked skin, an enormous mouth. In these cases there's no point saying to yourself it's all in your imagination, reason is left out of count and your imagination takes over.

Next day the two of them had lunch on the veranda again, and after their long meal they opened out two sun loungers and stretched down on them, covering themselves with a towel. Then began a whole series of sudden sharp noises, thundering sounds with brief pauses in between. I was taken aback for a while but then there was no room for ambiguity—the two of them were burping and farting, digesting shamelessly. I tried making light of it and laughing, but somehow I couldn't; now I knew that disgust would attach itself to my obsession, and as soon as that face appeared so close as to seem a horrific extension of my own, I knew that those thunderous roars would be dedicated to me as a grunting metaphor for his obscene desires.

Everyone has his own areas of rigidity, life imposes them on us, they must spring from the continual friction between the real world and the one that eludes us, fleeing from us. My own particular rigidity is intolerance towards anyone who thinks he can desire with impunity, taking advantage of an intimacy, even in the expression of his face, which does not belong to him. From that moment on, I felt myself to be in great danger.

That evening, I went down onto the road to throw away the rubbish. I had lifted the lid of the bin and that was why I had not heard the noise of the door opening behind me. I turned and saw him on the doorstep, in his pyjama bottoms, the lights on in the house and him even redder than I had seen him in his smile, turned a flaming red by the lighting and by his heavy drinking. He held a glass in his hand. He yelled into my face: Drink?

I just took off. I felt fear in my quivering legs, the way life has of fleeing to save itself when it is convinced of mortal danger. That night I didn't sleep a wink. I lay there listening and finding endless reasons for my fears, I really thought about leaving without even the shame of surrender. The next day I tried to get things a little more into perspective. I got up early and from the window I saw the slow pace of João Freitas setting off for his walk in the direction of Cabrito. It occurred to me to call out to him and tell him everything. He had known the man a long time and could certainly tell me something more about him, if there was anything to be afraid of, if he really was as monstrously awful as he appeared to me, or if he was just awful to look at and he was in fact as harmless as the vulgarity of his digestive farts. But the call never left my throat, it stayed nestling among the silent vocal chords. I could not get out as much as a whisper, not even that sigh which comes out breathless from our lips when we are about to fall asleep but our conscience is uneasy. Yet he felt something even from that distance, João Freitas, and he turned exactly to where I was looking at him, he saw me standing behind the windowpane and waved to me with the movement of his soft long arm that seems to be caressing a creature invisible or imaginary only to those who look at it. I answered his greeting with a barely perceptible movement of my hand, and thinking that somehow or other he could hear me, I said, Come back soon.

There was no point shutting myself up in the house, our fears are right there where we are, right where our bones join together, and under the first layer of skin where we can feel them chasing each other around and where we feel them liquid and coagulated, just like blood. I decided to take my fear out of the house, and I set off down the road for a natural swimming pool, a steep, tricky road of lava rock. I went down slowly, looking only where I was putting my feet, and that's why I didn't see him coming up slowly; I noticed him when there was no more than a single step between us. I saw his feet first without realising who they belonged to, and instinctively I moved aside to the left to make way for the person coming up. I saw him when we were on the same level. He had his towel over his shoulder, his skin was wet and a sort of shiny red, almost slimy, the few white hairs on his chest were curled into little dripping spirals and his face was monstrously wide, pushed outwards by a rigid smile, as if he had a walking stick shoved sideways inside his mouth. His eyes were clouded over like a great toad, and I think I said nothing because what my ears heard was the internal buzzing of my fear which was going crazy, something sticky which made the world fade a little around me. It was at that moment I felt the damp contact of his hand on my thigh, a light hold, almost as if he was leaning on me. I don't know how I got away, perhaps throwing myself down the steps, while terrible words were bursting inside my head, such as: You disgusting old man! Go and fart with your own wife!

And when we are running away there is great confusion in our thoughts, we don't know what we are saying anymore or what we are hearing, we don't even recognise our own voice, let alone what we are thinking. And so I don't know who answered me as I rushed down the steps as if I wanted to break my neck. I don't know if it was a real voice or just a thought, which could have been either mine or his, or which we could have both heard. But I remember what it said very clearly, it said: She's not my wife, she's my sister.

When I arrived at the natural pool, the last thing I felt like doing was going for a swim. I felt very cold, and could still feel the racing of my heart, which seemed to be doing its best to hammer out the little remaining life in it. Why are you so afraid, I asked myself, but then the more reasonable part of me told me to leave be; some questions have to be given free rein. I started to look out at the sea, which was calm and a lovely dark colour, and as often happens to me in moments of uncertainty, I trusted myself to destiny. Now I'll close my eyes and count slowly to ten, I thought. If when I open them again a seagull is flying in the sky that means I have nothing to fear. So that's what I did and that's what I saw, a seagull flying peaceably in almost immobile flight along the horizon; a scrap of silliness that calms my racing heartbeat, a game to play in order to rediscover my mind inside my body. In the pool, there were three little girls having a great time filling a big plastic drum with water and pouring it over themselves one at a time. As if they weren't wet enough already, I found myself thinking. And this is always a good sign, the fact that our mind doesn't stop, that it's quite capable of following a useless idea even when it is besieged by another one. I stood watching them with the zealousness of a sick man who studies his cure, and every peal of their laughter drew a long sigh from me, my hands resting on my hips and massaging the small of my back, because I know that this calms the nerves, something from here governs the brain and the neck muscles. I stood there watching those three little girls and I decided to follow their example. They are alive, I repeated to myself, and so I am alive too, and the beauty of this place is the great Atlantic vastness, the speed of the wind.

I waited until I began to feel a little better, then I began to climb back up the steps. When I reached the top of the cliff, I stopped at the tin shack, which was so small that not even the fridge could be squeezed inside and so the owner left it outside, covered by some matting held down by a stone. She had come back from America after almost thirty years, and since then, throughout the summer she sold ice creams and cold drinks and was kept company by four dogs, which wandered freely around the square. All they did was growl and snarl at each other in play. They stopped when she told them to be quiet, and when she called them, they dropped to the ground as if dead, subdued by a contented exhaustion.

I ordered a sweet peach liqueur and carried on standing by the counter, while the woman switched on a small neon light, ahead of the sunset. That was the time when the first workmen arrived from the yards of the tiny port in Cabrito; they stopped there before going home, to drink a beer in silence. Often they didn't even bother to switch off the engines of their battered vans, which they left just a little way off to shake in rusty shudders.

An old man used to bring a chair from his house and sit there the whole day covered in a straw hat. He looked at neither the sea nor the mountain; he let his eyes settle upon a horizon of rest, now and again he would whistle at the dogs, but without paying them any real attention. I drank the liqueur looking at the few bottles lined up inside the kiosk, reading the odd label here and there, and once or twice I felt the dampness of canine noses on the calf of my leg.

I went back home perfectly calm because fear is like that—sometimes it's so rancid that it brings to the surface all of its bad odours. Straight after dinner it started to rain, with the first nocturnal lament of the *cagarros,* who began looking for shelter. I went back into my house as well, thinking that it would be a good idea to go to bed early. I decided to draw that particular day to a close and I went to sleep easily enough.

I felt as if I was being woken in the middle of the night, but it can't have been much later because someone was knocking on my door, and these are not people who go around other people's houses if they think they might be disturbing them. When you wake suddenly you can have some strange reactions, sometimes you can think things that are utterly useless. It didn't occur to me to wonder who it might be, it seemed as if every part of my mind would be occupied with the fact that it was no longer raining. That's why I opened the door, because I sensed a change in the humidity, which I could feel at the base of my spine. So he came into my house saying something incomprehensible, and I wasn't even afraid, I just felt a stabbing pain at the back of my neck which produced a fit of coughing in me, and a tightening of the cheekbones at the level of my ears. He sat down in the kitchen, his hands twisting round and round a plate of figs, which he had brought me as a gift. What he had to say to me came out in a mixture of Portuguese and American, and what follows is what I understood him to be saying to me.

There must have been a misunderstanding, this often happens to ugly men of my age. I'm really sorry, I have come to apologise. It's an old story that has been going around for years; I should explain it first. Everyone has his cross to bear and others don't know about it. When you start to grow old it seems as though death is all there is left, as if old people can't think of anything else. I think very hard about other things. You know, thinking about death doesn't help very much, not even towards the end. Some people start to breathe more slowly in an attempt to stretch out their allotted time. It's a waste of time. And then at my age it almost always arrives in a way that does little damage, it is kind enough to creep in unnoticed and the person dying notices very little or even nothing. When I think of death I never think about my own, and I have come here just to tell you this story. Now I live with my sister, but when I was a young man in America, for four years I lived with my wife. A marriage that ended in divorce, like so many others. Two years ago, I found out that my wife had died. I knew two years ago but in fact she had passed away quite some time before, and this had a very strange effect on me. Though this isn't the story I wanted to tell you, but another one, and I don't want to sit here beating about the bush. When my wife fell pregnant she was very unhappy about it, she said it was foolish, but that she didn't want to have a child. I persuaded her to keep it, but I reckon a mother can do anything, somehow she holds the destiny of the child inside her in her hands. Our daughter was born premature, and she was born dead. Nothing will get it out of my head that this happened because her mother wanted it, she must have drunk something or she must have concentrated every effort of will to put the baby on the path to death. Afterwards we got divorced, and then I began to get this obsession: an obsession with counting the months and years of my daughter, as if she were alive. Now she would be the same age as you, a grown woman, and so sometimes I get these fixed ideas, especially when they seem to be sent by destiny, such as now with me coming back to Pico where I meet you, a foreigner on her own who also seems to have come here looking for someone. That's what obsessions are like: sometimes you can see them and sometimes they blind you. For the present, it's a moment of lucidity; tomorrow it will be who knows what, maybe the same as today on the steps, when I had a sudden urge to hold you. There is nothing else I can say to you. These figs are for you; the figs of Pico are famous for being the best in the world. Good night.

I stayed there in the kitchen looking at the decorated plate, which he had turned round and round in his hands the whole time. I was no longer sleepy, and so I ate three figs looking out at the night sky that held the promise of more rain. It was all clear now; he was quite a horrible man, but only for questions of digestion that I'd become used to by now. I listen to it after lunch, as at nighttime I listen to the blind lament of the *cagarros*, which fly in the dark. Apart from that we've become friends. I like watching him when he dives into the natural pool, his way of almost unconsciously making the sign of the cross before getting into the water. I didn't ask what his name was and I still don't know it. When I watch him or think about him I call him Drink.

Chapter seven

Isabel and
Maria José Lima

The house I see on my left is just a single storey, with a garden of lava rock and imported sand and from which sprouts the occasional self-seeded cactus. It was re-opened this year for the first time in sixteen years but it didn't take long for it to look the same way it always had in previous times, because if a woman on her own can work wonders, two women can work miracles, and when they bring three children with them it is as if they cancel out all traces of time. Sixteen years ago, the Lima sisters went to mix their blood in California. Isabel married an American of English origin, and Maria José married a Mexican. I've never managed to be objective as far as race is concerned, I much prefer the Latin peoples, and so Maria José's children seem to me far more beautiful than Isabel's only child. But what I really appreciate about all the children as a whole is their seriousness, the respect with which they explore this land. I've noticed that only the two women sleep in the house, the children have made themselves a refuge almost on the edge of the cliff. They must have had a hard job carrying all those blocks of black stone, and for the roof they chose the most rudimentary means possible—cardboard boxes and old woollen blankets, held in place by other big stones. They sleep down there whatever the weather and in the evening, before going off to bed, they light a good strong fire, which from where I am, seems to be rising out of the sea.

As often happens, the Lima sisters are completely different one from the other. Maria José is a beautiful, silent woman who spends her time reading enormous novels, her back leaning against the rocks of the cliffs, and shaded by a huge straw hat. Sometimes I see her walking with her children, but even then she doesn't seem to have much desire to speak. She walks without paying much attention to where she is putting her feet, drawn by the beauty of the sky, often taking her hat off to take a better look at it. Seen in this way she looks like a very serene woman, and I've become attached to the idea that she is a woman who really is happy.

Isabel can't have been beautiful even as a young woman, she has the square body of a brick-layer and the long face of a sea perch, and a way of moving her mouth that makes you think large bubbles of air and water should come out of it. On her broad shoulders she carries the weight of a life that has been led saying too many things that can't have been understood. I've always thought there can't be any other explanation for someone who never tires of talking. Besides, Isabel is the one married to the man originally from England, and as far as I can see there's no way out when that is the situation. Latin blood joined with Nordic blood doesn't seem to me a good idea, for the Latin I mean, because the Nordic one is the winner, he gains a little fire, but in return he gives only a great dampening which gradually stifles the other one. I would say that Isabel came back to the island after sixteen years in order not to die, because in her heart, like every red-blooded animal, she felt the danger that was threatening her, and she wasn't ready to give up yet.

Some people have to live alone in order to regenerate themselves, but Isabel needed to bring her sister along with her because sometimes it is difficult to regenerate, we need a lot of paraphernalia.

They had been together here on the island when they were children, and the past is not something that can be put back together just like that, you need to proceed with great sensitivity and fleetness of foot. That is why the presence of the two women was not enough, and it was absolutely essential to have the boys in the background. I met Isabel one morning when she was alone in her house, at the time when the milk van generally comes around. She was in the garden rinsing out the metal jug and as she turned round she saw me reading on the veranda. Being one of those people who is scared of being alone with her own thoughts, she spoke to me, addressing me with the usual question which so neatly dissolves the distance between two strangers. She raised her fish-like snout to me and asked: Do you like it here?

I answered that I liked it very much and she dried her hands on her dress with the hasty movements of someone who doesn't want to miss their chance. She came over and leant her elbows on the low wall that separated her house from mine. Seen from this distance she was less ugly than from far off, but this could be because of my liking for fish, my habit of always regarding them with indulgence when I see them dangling from a hook, even when the hook is mine.

Perhaps living here doesn't seem so easy to you, she said, moving her freckly cheeks, and I limited myself to the gesture of someone who agrees and dissents at the same time, because it was perfectly obvious that I wasn't the one who was to do the talking. She stood there under the sun which was pressing down on her still florid skin, her half closed eyes staring intently at me. And so I gave her all the space and time she wanted.

"Do you know how long it was since I'd been back? Sixteen years. It takes my breath away thinking about it, sixteen years seems longer now than it did before I left. When we are far away we just keep putting everything off whether it's the past or the future, they both just slip away, move off to the side. I arrived two months ago with my sister and I said to myself, Isabel, you've grown old and you didn't even notice. In a country which isn't yours, you don't know what you are anymore, you stay the same as when you arrived, you look for what is definitive and you only find what is provisional. You ask yourself, how long can this go on for? And it goes on for years, as in a long sleep. There is something that goes to sleep, and do you know what it is? It is abandonment. The danger is when we wake up again, there are strange smells, but not those of a closed up room, they are new odours that you have never smelled before and at this distance I can smell them now, I can smell the smells of California. It's not that my life is bad over there; I can't say that hand on heart. Everything looks lovely here in Pico now, but the winter is miserable, rain, rain and more rain, nothing but wind and rain. With the weather here your hairdo is in pieces in a matter of minutes. And I've got a good job over there, I'm a teacher. I didn't do what they call here *dar o salto*, take a leap in the dark, I didn't go there as an immigrant, I married a man I met in Portugal, an American. There are things we don't notice when they are right under our noses. Do you know what I did then? I took my little sister with me; she's five years younger than me. I thought she might be able to study in a new country. Do you know what I mean? Now everything is clear, but at the time I couldn't see it, everything was floating, like air. No woman in the world gets married and then takes her sister with her. If I had had eyes to see inside myself, I would never have left, but eyes are strange things, they see and they are blind at the same time. I've brought my sister along with me again this time, and our children too. But our lives were very different even though we've always been together, because life is very much a matter of our feelings and we were both lucky women, but not in ways that match up together very well. Does that seem strange to you? My view is that there is a material happiness, and a verbal one, and another one that is both these things together. Mine has been a happiness in the words of others. And I felt this to be true for year after year, in a vast, bewildered, sort of way, for the whole time that I refused to face up to facts and be realistic. Did you know that illusion lasts for at least half of our entire life? Have you never heard that? Realism has to do with our independence, living slightly apart, as if nothing was ours anymore and belonged instead to heaven only knows whom. Only then do we emerge from our illusion, when we enter the solitude that encircles the world. The works of artists provide a good example of this… Have you ever noticed how everybody, even the best critics, says that the mature works are the best? That's nonsense, it comes from looking just at the surface, the aggression you see when they are young springs from their participation in the world, in their illusion. After, when they give up, they seem better people, but it is the cruel goodness of the old man who laughs and weeps alone, who invents for himself a world of abstract sweetness now that disenchantment and a heavy dose of realism suggest to him the luxury of absolute fantasy. We are never truly realist, that is the lesson of art which is always unreal because life gets in the way too much.

You, too, I don't suppose you've come all this way here for nothing, have you? Life gets too much in the way, it's too solid. Nowadays, my whole life seems to me to have been an illusion. As the years have gone by I've distanced myself too, and now I look at everything with different eyes, including my sister. People have always said about us that I was the one who was happy and open to the world while she was the quiet one, closed up in hers. But hers was beautiful, not like mine where I was groping around blindly. Now that we're here together, we are enjoying the island with all its distant memories, and my sister does it with her way of being apart from things which takes everything and then manages to leave it in its place; not like me—I have to latch on like a short-lived insect. I can already see our return back to California, she will talk about it a lot to her husband, whole evenings, a whole new passion will come out of it. I will say nothing to mine. Coming here has been the most awesomely terrible thing I could have done to myself, as if I have dug out the emptiness of my own future. I told you before that winter here is very sad, but that's not what I was thinking, here I can find the winter of my past, my land, my whole life which I should not have abandoned. I would have been a more authentic person if I'd stayed living here, I would have married one of these local men so rich in melancholy and we would have exchanged our thoughts even in silence.

Have you been to the fiesta of Cabrito? It's on for a long time yet, you really ought to go. A square in semi-darkness with three houses perched on the edge of the cliff, a shack where they sell *favas guisadas* and roast kid with potatoes, *licor de amora* and *anis* with a crystallized twig inside the bottle, then there's the little platform in the middle of the square where they play the *chamarrita*, and the kiosk in the shape of a whale where they do the lottery.

Do you know what, I met my first love there the other night. His name was Pedro Nuñes and he made me fall in love with him just with his long, sideways glances at me as I hurried along the paths through the vineyards to take my father his lunch. We never spoke to each other, just the day before I left he came under my window and looked at me. Only then did I feel the desire to hear his voice and I asked him: What do you want to say to me?

It must have been the darkness of the night, but he was intensely pale, like someone who has just died, and with the voice of the spirits he said to me, Nothing, only that, if you leave tomorrow, you will never come back.

And then he went away, leaving me chilly with fear, because those are not the words you want to hear when you are about to leave, and I was just going to the mainland to study, it was a journey which in its beginning already had an end. But the ideas we have in our heads don't count for very much, my mother used to say that making plans was just a way of unmaking them. Would you believe me if I said that I forgot Pedro Nuñes as soon as I arrived in Portugal? That's what it's like being young, distractions cover over our memories like icing sugar. And Lisbon seems put together with the intention of making you forget the rest of the world. I lived on the Avenida de Libertade and as I hurried down it in the morning I really did feel like another person, ravished by that sky. I never thought about him again until I met him the other evening at Cabrito. And yet I must have thought about him a lot, thought about him so much I didn't realise it, do you know what I am saying? These are the strange games our soul plays, and it's just the same as with secrets that involve us very closely, we are always the last to find them out. I saw him eating *favas guisadas* with his wife and four children. I looked at him with the same jumping heartbeat as when I used to run through the vineyards, but he didn't recognise me; he was eating and drinking *vinho de cheiro* with the look of someone who is serene to the point of happiness. And then I said to myself that I must have become an ugly old American if he really didn't realise that it was me. My sister asked me: What's the matter, aren't you well?

But I just shook my head, moving my upper body a little as well, the way we do when a shiver of cold runs over us. I answered her, it's the humidity, it's too humid this evening. But really it was that first love which came hurtling back, breaking the banks and dams of the years like a great nail in the middle of my chest, a sudden rush of blood. I could have said I'm dying, or else I'm being born, but of course we are never born at this age, we can only die, and I'll maybe take my whole old age to do it. We are going back to California in two weeks time. Maria José is already thinking about coming back here with her husband, and I'm sure he'll say how lovely her land is, that at times it reminds him of his own. It's different for the two of them, they are both living in a foreign land and this brings them closer together in the fantasy of memory. You know what the real joke is? That in some ways I've warmed the Nordic coldness of my husband, and if you were to ask him how it's been he would say it has been a good life. But never forget it, an Englishman is an Englishman wherever he happens to be born. Well, the sting in the tail is that when one side takes over another, it is itself weakened and impoverished, it's like decanting wine, the demijohn fills up the bottle and is emptied in the process, and it's as a poor woman that I'll be going back to California—I'll be totally wretched now that I have seen Pedro Nuñes again. And this time I won't have the dark side of my conscience to help me forget, because this time the greater part of my life has already gone by, and when there's not much more we can expect, we go back to what really counts. This island is stunningly beautiful. Before I leave, I want to climb the mountain on foot, right to the top. The last time I did it I must have been fifteen or sixteen years old, with my father and my sister. If it's a fine day from up there you can see Faial and São Jorge, Graciosa as well, but it has to be an absolutely clear day with no wind. I hope I'll be lucky enough to take that memory away with me, because I don't think it's likely I'll be coming back here. I reckon this really will be the last time I breathe the air of Pico, the air of my youth and of Pedro Nunes.

It's done me a lot of good to talk to you, you know, I feel as if I'm almost content. Perhaps that means I'm still not entirely lucid, that I'm not yet old enough to weep and laugh all by myself, like the great artist in his mature works. Perhaps I'll never be that way. If right to the end I stay in love with Pedro Nunes, there's a good chance I'll manage to rescue myself from the emptiness of grief, from the great intolerance that makes us seem superficially tolerant. I must have been wrong when I told you that coming here was the greatest harm I could possibly have done myself, but life is one whole contradiction and sometimes contradictions can have something to teach us. Perhaps I'll find that my Englishman waiting for me in California has become just a little less English, but if that really does happen, I'll write you a postcard and you must promise me you'll keep it as a relic, proof of an extraordinary event. It's a real shame I'm leaving so soon now—we could have been friends, I would have got you to meet my sister who is a walking study of how to be happy, and our three hardy boys who've been sleeping over there near the cliff edge whatever the weather. My God, how I've been chatting on, I must be really unhappy, like a flower that has faded but does not realise it, as the poem says. You've been very kind to listen to me for so long. Maybe you think I'm plain mad, or maybe you've just been poking fun at me. No? Just as well, nobody likes to think their sorrow is providing entertainment for someone else. That means you really have been very kind, as silent as my sister, maybe you are happy just as she is. It's not true that our own sorrow makes us kinder to other people, look at me, I talk and I never listen to anybody, I talk and that's all. After we'd been married two months my husband said to me: But are you never quiet? I answered him that he was so quiet that life would go totally untold. But it made no difference, you know? Words in the wind, and there's plenty of wind in California too. Who knows who has listened to all those words of mine, certainly not him. It's just occurring to me that Pedro Nuñes might have listened to them. That would be nice, don't you think? Yes, really nice, with my voice reaching him, and him saying to himself, I can hear you but I cannot see you and I would like to see you so much. His embraces would have been warm; men from around these parts are virile in a very emotional way. Take João Freitas, his wife dead, poor thing, and now he has nothing left except the love of memories, the complete happiness of his time with her. It will never occur to him to look for another woman, he will stay faithful to her in this new way, but this won't make him feel any the less male than those who on the contrary need a bit of company. He will still have the sentimental side of his life, and that will always seem enough to him. You're free now, I shan't say another word. The milkman's coming; he's late today. If you haven't tried it yet, you should buy a litre of milk from him. The cows have only just been milked, it's lovely—you can still taste the grass. I'll say goodbye.

⁊₭

During the two weeks that were left, we only ran into each other briefly a few times, but we understood each other. It was only when she left that she paid me a proper visit, and she brought me a soup of wild herbs and *pancetta*. We swapped addresses. Maybe I'll be sending you that postcard after all, she said smiling at me, and then she spent the rest of the day in her house packing.

It was Drink who took them to the airport, because he had a car. The three boys got in first, then Maria José, dressed with the strange elegance of the Americans, shaded by her hat even on a cloudy day like that. Isabel was last to get in, going around saying goodbye to everyone and giving everyone endless hugs. I would like

71

to have gone out into the street to say goodbye to her, but I would have been out of place, the only foreigner amidst all those sad emigrants. When she turned in my direction, I made the only gesture that came to mind. I lifted my hand to my hair and twisted it round my finger. I don't know if she was smart enough to understand; with all my heart, I was wishing her chic and lasting hairdos. There was not much to wish for Maria José, just a few hours on and she would be rediscovering her Mexican passion intact.

The house reverted to the same solitude in which it had remained for sixteen years, a few beach towels were left hanging out to dry in the wind of an afternoon which promised nothing but rain. They certainly didn't belong to the two sisters; they'd borrowed them from kind people for whom someone from the same land was like a member of the family. Whoever owned them would go and collect them as soon as they were dry.

Chapter eight

João Vieira Freitas

There are exceptions everywhere, even amongst those who, to 'make the leap,' generally choose the new continent. Some are suddenly overtaken by a sudden urge and go off following a rhythm of their lives that springs from some sort of impatience. Others are dreamers and carry their dreams in their eyes, which by dint of contemplating their dream turn a beautiful clear blue. These are strange people who prefer to resonate with their own thoughts, and you can often tell them from their voices, voices which speak high and completely alone, discoursing with the night and the luminous sky. This has nothing to do with madness, as they understand full well here, it is simply a form of extravagance that runs counter to the norm.

If you ask him about it he replies with his radiant smile, *Je m'sui di pourqua l'Amerique? Pourqua si tous y von?* The clearness of his gaze, always ready and waiting, is remarkable, with its almost witless transparency, which fixes emptiness and perhaps colours it. He says with a laugh that he likes to introduce himself as João Freitas, and then he adds João Vieira Freitas, and that's the end of his little joke. Then he lights a cigarette and waits for the person he's talking to ask, any relative of João Freitas? Then he replies, satisfied, he's my cousin, we have almost exactly the same name, and his cheeks crack into two absolutely straight parallel lines, beautiful in the colour of flesh.

Here he is the only person who emigrated to France and he's proud of it. Twenty years of profound transformation, he's almost French now with that sibilant way he has of speaking, his words airy and ventilated, perhaps this is the reason that there is not an ounce of fat on him. A slender man, then, ageless, his skin hardened and dehydrated by a constant thought process which nobody looking at him would call rational but which is crowded, jostling. His turbulent thinking has deprived him of sleep.

The first time I saw him, he was driving an ancient little scooter and he had half a cigarette dangling from the right side of his mouth. Hanging on behind him was the skinniest of old ladies, like a hallucination, a trick of the light that made her out to be all shadow. Her ghostly pallor was striking, and it was enough to make you think that he was taking around a ghost who must have been very dear to him. He was going slowly along the road to Cachorro, leaving in his wake a swathe of red dust, which looked like a comet. Seen like that, with the sunset at his back, he looked like a low-flying bird.

He almost always appeared as evening was drawing in, and in the house where I was living. This was clear right from the start, for João Freitas had told me that I would hear some noise from the floor below, since his cousin had the keys to the cellar where they kept the wine and the *angelica*. He would arrive, slowly, on foot, as the sun was going down, when the sky grows dark and everyone is assembled inside for dinner—the time of day when the Arcos road seems to consume itself in the ample breathing of the earth which makes it seem narrower.

You knew he was arriving because you could hear his voice, his way of greeting the absent world, almost a talking cough. I could hear him fiddling around in the cellar, where perhaps he lingered over a solitary drink, talking all the time, saying things sonorous in tone, saying without speaking. I loved to listen to him, and I would lie down on the floor to hear him better. I speak French well, and what was remarkable in João Vieira Freitas was that even his indistinct mumbling voice imitated the other language, even when some word came out in Portuguese. I stayed glued to the floor as long as he was down there; I only got up when I heard him about to leave. Then I would look out of the window to see him, to watch him walking back home like a drunk, in his hand the demijohn brimming full of wine for dinner and for lunch the following day.

I'm convinced that he wouldn't have wanted to meet me if he hadn't known that to make a living I teach French. Here at Arcos, I told him, I'm known as *la italiana profesora de frances*. And this must have jogged his memory somehow; it must have brought back to mind long forgotten fantasies, things from his own time, which had nothing to do with me. Indeed, with João Vieira Freitas I had the impression of being a memory, that when I was in front of him I was there and not there at the same time, or perhaps I was there too much. Be that as it may, he came to see me one morning, breaking all of his habits, dressed with the starched care of simple men. I was in the house, although it was ten o'clock by now, and I heard him cough a few words in a quiet voice as I was going up my stairs. He didn't knock as I opened the door, and once he was inside he held out his hand to offer me a bottle of *angelica*.

C'est pour vous, he said, his blue eyes shining full of seawater, as if they were crying.

I don't know how they do things around here, but in my zeal to find out I uncorked the bottle and said we would drink a glass of it together. João Vieira Freitas began to laugh, and his hand described the rapid movement of someone rubbing out a word wrongly written. That wasn't the time of day to be drinking *angelica*, what sort of person was I to be drinking liqueurs in the morning? He stood there on the veranda, waiting for me to come out of the house. This much I had learnt, that a man and a woman met outside where any passer-by could see, and say: Everything's in order, it's just a courtesy visit. I told him I would be out straight away; I would just make a coffee if he would like one. He lit a cigarette and stayed outside, still standing, leaning against a column, in the light wind of a clear day with just a few wispy clouds.

The first few minutes of our meeting passed thus, drinking our coffee in silence, greeted by Malvina Sebastião who was hanging out her washing. I said to myself, he'll finish his coffee now and then he'll be on his way; but on the contrary, he remained in his seat (he made not the slightest move to get up) and offered me a cigarette. His conversation was all in emigrant's French, the most beautiful French I have ever heard, lightly shaded by his mother tongue, which now and then rendered it slow and persuasive, then cavernous and flooded. His use of grammar was plucked from his imagination, and I was particularly struck by his almost obsessive choice of the word *pourquoi*, which he used for why, so that, since, then, hardly and who knows how many other meanings that I never caught. He laughed at the idea that I might teach that language, and he explained his theory that it is impossible to learn something when someone is teaching it.

C'est tout perdu, he said, but when I asked him what it was that was lost he replied, *J'été bien en France*, and he drifted off into memories that excluded the present.

Our talk was full of long silences, and often I felt as though I was absent, but this was never a cause of embarrassment. I was incapable of bringing to mind anything that affected me alone; I just waited for him to return to this world and begin talking again.

There are people who become more beautiful in their old age. When you look at them, you wonder what rare beauty they had as young people. But there is nothing to seek behind, they are beautiful now, now that they are near the end but still vigorous. If you looked at him closely, João Vieira Freitas was a sumptuous man; when he sat down, he naturally took up the position of a Portuguese statue in the centre of a square, in trance-like composure. Perhaps this is because he had lived elsewhere for so long and had then come back; there was a great decency in the return, a considered and at the same time modest absorption. He came back here to live in the clarity and grace of his thoughts, and settle down again in his own way.

Vous l'savé pourqua je sui parti? Simple, c'est pourqua de la langue.

Not simple at all, I answered, I don't understand.

He clapped his hands, clapped them in excitement. But of course it's simple, every language has its own sound, we are attracted to them as birds are attracted when the hunter calls them with that whistle of his. That's why nobody could teach a language to somebody else, because it is the language itself that gives out its own appeal.

Vous pensé c'est rêve? On rêve toujours, c'est question d'humanité. On est humain pourqua on rêve.

What an extraordinary thing to say, I said, you are an extraordinary man, signor João Vieira Freitas. I could choose to believe him or not, but he had gone to France attracted by the musical sound of the language. Like a migrating bird crosses the seas when the season changes with the arrival of the first winter chills, he'd gone in search of some warmth. And just as birds know that they will find a warm sun, he knew that when he arrived over there he would speak the language and everybody would understand him.

C'est comme ça pour l'émigrant, personne le lui apprend, pourqua il apprend tout seul avec l'idée qu'il en avé avant. C'est tout dans l'idée s'on le garde.

Not bad at all for somebody who has learnt by himself, precise and concise like the thought of a man from ancient times. I told him that the thing I liked best about the Azores was that they were all so strangely ancient. He answered that this was the case because that was what I was seeking, and that's why I liked being there so much, because there are things, he said, lowering his voice, which we feel so strongly inside that we can't miss. What about disappointments? I asked him. Those make their nest in the rafters, he said, rubbing his hands, and there is no dream or journey that is of any use to them. They no sooner leave than they come back again. Life without dreaming is life with never any peace.

It was true. The sound had been enough for him, there had never been any disappointment in it, while he was over there, his face set against the wind of the port of Saint-Guenolé, unloading containers of fish, and while the sheds resounded with the crashing noise of the high-speed jets of water, which washed away the purplish blood and slippery remains with a force so powerful that it silenced the sea. He had been content just with the thought of that language, with his deep thought of it.

His destination was the act of leaving itself, I told him. Everybody else went instead to the new world.

C'est pas vré, on part toujours avec une destination, il y a du projet dans la vie, pourqua, s'il y en a. Là-bas, en Amerique, y a pas de langue et pour moi pas de destination. They say time passes quickly, but that's not exactly true. It's true in the present, sometimes, but in memory it stretches out to infinity, and to João Vieira Freitas those twenty years seemed at least two or three lifetimes put together. These are the tricks of memory and solitude, a fixed idea which, when it becomes an obsession, takes away even our sleep. Over there he felt there was no time to waste, while here time seemed bewildering to him. He tried to summon up some special memory, but he had done nothing special, had been absorbed by nothing for twenty years, with no time even for a fleeting love, but all the same absorbed to the roots of his being. Always alone in the midst of all those seagulls lined up on top of the sheds to beg some leftover scraps. Proudly he tells me the name of the town again, Saint-Guenolé, near Concarneau, in Brittany. Inspector Maigret's patch he said, laughing, and posing as an inspector just by turning up the lapel of his jacket. That had been his real passion over there, he'd read all the books and was still re-reading them.

C'est pour le son, vous savé, faut pas oublier.

So João Vieira Freitas was a reader of Simenon, and he had carried on reading him now that he was back in Pico. He, indeed, might have been one of those who don't come back, still strolling along the quay of Brittany with its long sunsets and the strong smell of dark red seaweed which piles up high on the beach and which fishermen collect as a precious gift. And I wondered if his return to Pico has been another destination in life, another dreamed sound. He looked at me, and I knew what he was thinking, he was thinking that I would never teach anything to anyone. And maybe he was right; there is no sound that can be taught.

So why did you come back? I asked, without noticing that I had slipped into *tu*, into the familiar form of address. Sorrow made him lift his chin skywards and I saw his long throat, that human slope which expresses all of our emotions. He opened the palms of his hands on his thighs, opened them to the sun that lights them as they rest there, in the ripples of time, where the times of life and death are inscribed.

Profesora, he said, when I talk about the present I have to talk in my own language. You know what I mean, don't you? There are no ideas of sound in the present, only old age. Mine has barely begun but that of my parents was coming to an end and I couldn't just abandon them. I'm the only one of their children who doesn't have a family of my own, the others are all far away, and so it was down to me to come and watch them fade slowly away. I said my farewells to the great fish containers which I used to unload before sundown, and right to the last I was tempted to take one away with me to remind myself how beautiful they were, in heavy plastic, in muted colours of white and grey, with lovely writing on the side with the port code and all the rest. I was always moved by them, scratched about inside by the shoals of those enormous mud-coloured Atlantic fish, pock-marked by the ice which is packed around them. Later on, when the wholesale buyers arrived, the containers were put to march slowly along those conveyor belts like the ones you see in airports to carry your baggage away, each one with its price written on a square of white paper, turned crumpled and transparent by the dampness of the fish. But I couldn't take one away with me, they were too big, and anyway it wasn't allowed. My father is almost ninety and I have to do everything for him, even spoon-feed him like a baby. He's leaving slowly, with that way old people have of looking around them terrified, as if they can see something unknown which they can't even tell you about. We can't have any idea what is going on inside their heads; they're between two worlds, and they see a bit of this one and a bit of the next. That's the price you pay for living a long time, that's how they end up, in enormous fear. My mother couldn't manage alone; she's old and as thin as a ghost. When she looks at herself in the mirror, she always sighs at the idea of her consumption, and sometimes she tells me. I'm disintegrating into tiny pieces, my son, every night death robs me of another piece even as I sleep.

For their sake, I abandoned my containers of fish and the sound of French which I never finished learning, just as I would never have finished learning it had I stayed, because nothing ever really comes to an end in this life. Now I'm sometimes afraid of becoming a man with no sound, but that's just foolishness, and you must understand that, because you will never forget the sound of this earth when you go back to your own, isn't that right? But perhaps you won't go back. Maybe you will decide to stay here and hear it echoing. Sound is everything, did you realise that? It comes by and then comes by again. In other places people would think I was mad, but only where there is no sea, because by living near it you learn its sound. Perhaps one day I'll go back to France *où j'été si bien. Vous savé, j'été moi même un poisson parmi les poissons. C'été l'elevation, la joie d'etr loin. Je parle bien mantenan, pas si bien can j'été loin. Alor je vulé apprendr, mantenan je sé. Vous connessé le son de la mort? Quelquefois c'est teleman ravissan madame, ça vous parle. Vous n'avé rien à apprandr par les otres, n'ublié pas. Il ne fo qu'ecuté.*

Maybe it wasn't the right time of day to be drinking *angelica*, but we ended up by finishing the whole bottle, and I don't remember what else João Vieira Freitas said to me, nor do I remember what language he used to express his restless thoughts. Now we are great friends. During the day, when he goes by on his ancient motorbike to take his mother to the *minimercado* in Santa Luzia, he never fails to slow down when he reaches my house. If he sees me on the veranda he waves with the briefest of gestures of his right hand, which he takes off the handlebars just for a moment. His mother turns towards me as well, with her thin face which even from the front looks as though it is in profile, and she gives me a quick, pallid wave.

You were lucky to have a son who has come back, I say to her in my mind, every time I see her. You will have someone to close your eyes with love. And now I think that João Vieira Freitas will also be placing flowers on her grave, since he is no longer of an age to go off in pursuit of a sound. Things consume themselves, even illusions, or, who knows, perhaps they just change person.

Chapter nine
Cabrito

I wanted to follow Isabel Lima's advice. I asked João Freitas to lend me a torch and from Arcos I set out on foot as far as Cabrito, along the road which hugs the coastline and which would be dark as soon as I was out of the area that had *luz publica*. She had said I shouldn't miss the fiesta and I wanted to do as she suggested, at least out of homage to her, as by now she had gone back to California to a house which must have been so utterly different from the one she had abandoned here, and to the comfortless arms of her English husband.

It was a beautiful night with a warm wind, and I know by now that this is not a place where you have anything to fear, because the people here are still living in those times which have never existed; times of peace. The lava coast followed me round with its human shapes of people shipwrecked and turned to stone, women and men astonished by the enchantment of the sea to the point of forgetting that they had been saved. The never total darkness made it easier to recognise them as in a game, and as I passed by in front of the priest's house, I let the tales of Malvina Sebastião linger in my mind,

and I really did seem to see the man from other times who was like
a plant, and who appeared only to those who wished to see him. We
greeted each other with a polite wave of the hand. He was leaning
against the dry stone wall of the house, dressed like a peasant going
to a public holiday, and when I was a few steps past him, he began
whistling the tune of a *chamarrita*, which I had often heard drifting
out from the house of my friend Drink. So I turned to look back at
him, so tiny that he looked like a little old baby, and I saw he had
raised his arms in the gentle movement of that ancient dance. Why
don't you come with me to the fiesta? I asked him. As he began to
trace a few steps of the dance he answered, without looking at me:
I can't, I've put too many roots down here; you go and have a good
time for me too.

As I walked along I told myself I must have an overactive
imagination if I was starting to talk to the plants. But that was an
excuse for not turning back, because I could still hear the whistling
all the while, and the night was heavily scented.

From a distance, Cabrito appeared weakly lit up for the occasion by numerous generators, and at the entrance to the village visitors were welcomed by a goat tied to a tree. There can't have been
more than fifteen people in the square in groups of two or three,
chatting quietly. If it hadn't been for the smell of the *favas guisadas* and the meat stew, both of which were served from behind an
improvised counter, it would never have occurred to me that there
was a festival going on. I went up to an old man sitting on a step at
the edge of the square.

Have I got here too late? I asked.

On the contrary, he answered, it hasn't got going yet. If you
haven't eaten you can eat here, there's some excellent kid stew with
potatoes and *bolo de milord.* And be sure not to miss the draw, if you
are lucky there are still some lovely prizes left.

I didn't feel like eating. I felt too much as though I was waiting in an emotional suspense, that something was still missing. I was
sitting on the low wall of the tiny port of Cabrito looking partly at
the still absent festival, partly at the slope down to the sea behind

me, black now that night had completely fallen, touched with silver by the brief appearances of the moon. In the square, the generator light lent the few people around a yellowish colour, which made them look doughy and transparent at the same time, empty around the eyes, which had almost vanished.

A man came to sit next to me, balancing on his knees a plate with the kid stew and potatoes. Aren't you eating anything? he said. I shook my head to say no, as if I didn't know how to speak anymore.

That's no good, he said. You don't come to a festival just to watch. Anyway, this is a speciality that we have just a few days each year. And as he said that he came up closer, wriggling his bottom along the wall, and from close up he seemed to have no colour at all, just the pale blue of his veins, his eyes shining bright like large pools of light. I don't even know if they were light or dark.

At least try a bit of this delicious meat, a mouthful won't kill you.

And so he put a piece onto his own fork, poking around in his plate to find the best bits, and he offered it to me without even thinking that I might not appreciate such intimacy. I didn't have much time to think, and so I ate from his plate under a sky which was turning starry at our backs, not in front of us. In front of us all we could see was the weak light of the generators and the sky completely black, as if we were living in two nights at the same time. And so we continued to eat together like brother and sister, very comfortable with each other.

Who are you waiting for? he asked me. Who knows, maybe some people from Arcos, I expected to find them here.

Do you know many of them?

Yes, João Freitas, Malvina Sebastião, Maria Moniz, an elderly man here with his sister, I don't know his name, João Vieira Freitas, the one with the parents who are old and sick, two sisters who have already gone back to California…

He placed his hand on my shoulder and said: They'll come. You'll see, they'll be here.

Now I imagine you'll want to tell me your story too, I said. You will tell me about your experience as an emigrant, how you left and then came back. That's all I've been hearing since I arrived.

He shook his head sadly and caressed the knuckles of my hand.

I won't tell you any story, he said. I haven't told any story for a while now. I like the fact that you are a foreigner, I like sitting here next to you, eating this goat meat together now that the festival is starting.

But what sort of festival is this? I asked. When on earth does it start? There's no hurry, here things go as they must go, very slowly, and when it does start don't go expecting too much, they'll open the draw kiosk (if I may I would like to buy you a ticket) and then they'll get around to playing a *chamarrita* or two and there will be few who are happy enough to get up and dance after all the wine they'll have put away. Don't worry, I don't have a life to tell you, only things to forget.

Then tell me one of them while we are waiting, I said, trying to get him to look at me. Impossible, signora.

And, so saying, he stretched out on the wall, resting his head in my lap and shutting his eyes. Don't go to sleep, I said. If you sleep the damp will go right into your bones.

It doesn't matter, he replied, but who knows who he was talking to, he was already drifting off and so I lifted up his head and left him there to sleep like a man who is perfectly content. Nobody seemed bothered by the wait, some were eating and drinking, taking plates and glasses away with them, others were eating off the counter, as if at a manger. Almost eleven o'clock. That's not a time for festivals to begin in a tiny forgotten place like this; by this time festivals are well finished. I was thinking this as I sat on a bench made of lava stone, looking at the divided sky. Two worlds up there as well, I thought, the stars all out at sea, the hill vanished in the night, or the thick darkness. Perhaps I should go, and just as I was thinking that, a door opened and out of a house came six children dressed in white and accompanied by an elderly woman.

86

Who are they? I asked her.

The players.

At last. I was about to leave, I told her; I thought this festival was an illusion. Is it really going to start?

Soon, she said, the children have to eat first.

She sat them on the steps of the church, each with their beret next to them. They were served by the man who cooked behind the counter, and they ate slowly, with the timid care of someone not used to wearing white. They all finished at the same time, mopping up the sauce with slices of *bolo de milho*, the cake-like bread, and stayed sitting down.

What else are we waiting for now? I asked the woman.

The guitars, she answered, just the guitars, then we will begin.

Just at that moment, the draw kiosk opened up, emitting a feeble light, and I saw a girl round as an egg, who'd been hiding away until now, shut inside maybe with the prizes, soft and rosy as a suckling pig. She looked out, leaning her ample, youthful bosom on a wooden ledge damp with the humidity. I went up to see. There were bizarre things, ancient things, as João Freitas would have said with pride. The girl stretched out what little neck she had: You have a free ticket, she said softly.

I answered that I was not surprised and turned towards the wall where I had left a man sleeping. He's gone, the girl said, he said he didn't want to stay any longer, he was tired. And then her gaze left me to fix itself on the middle of the square where the six players were standing up, their guitars in their hands. I've got number 306, I said. She rummaged amongst the many things hanging up, as if looking for what came to hand.

You're lucky, she said, it's a lovely lace table-centre, all hand-made.

But she wasn't paying me any attention as she gave me the prize, and immediately after she left the kiosk to go into the middle of the square. You come too, she said, as she moved away, it's the *chamarrita*! But I stood where I was, wrapped up in my own thoughts, in the amazement of those who stay outside of things, because I couldn't see any more people there, still the same fifteen or so, yet now that they were dancing the first one I saw was João Freitas with the smooth skin of bygone youth, and then his cousin João Vieira Freitas with the shining eyes which one day would see the land destined to call him with its strange sounds. They were both staring with identical passion at a girl I knew too. I saw her in a photograph, and time made her the wife of just one of them, who took her off to California.

That was a fine story you told me, João Vieira Freitas, I said to him, going up to him as he was dancing.

You didn't go off to hear a sound at all, you went away so as not to hear the voice of jealousy.

Instead of answering, he looked at me.

It doesn't matter my friend, I said, nobody knows the memories of the future. But as I said it, he was changing a little before my eyes, as if growing old. Just as a bit further over, Malvina Sebastião was old as she danced without feeling the pain in her back, those wide movements of her arms almost certainly for my benefit, while her high, masculine voice was telling everybody when they should change their step and all the women go into the circle.

You're here and you're not here, I thought, looking at them. But Isabel Lima, dancing together with her sister, told me that they were there indeed.

But you two left, I said without much conviction. I saw you leaving; the two of you really must be a hallucination. But Isabel Lima just laughed at that: It's the power of thought, she said, emerging from the dancing. Have you forgotten the power of thought? Reality is not a thing we all see in the same way, everyone fashions it as he wants. But don't ask me now if we are here because we want to be, or if it is a trick of your own mind, because you'd spoil all my fun, and this is not a night for wasting time, so just let it be for now.

I told her that she must be right, that hers was a lovely idea, but in my heart of hearts I know I had grounds for being puzzled, because seeing or not seeing hardly counts for more than we know.

And I mused that the power of thought was indeed very strong, but that the two of them were nevertheless back in California, one happy and the other full of regret.

Stop these endless ruminations on your rational silliness, she said, taking my hand. See that guy over there drinking beer? That's Pedro Nuñes, and another life is beginning for me here, even though it might last only one night. So don't stand there thinking we are in California, or you'll spoil everything! Come dance the *chamarrita* with us.

I can't dance, I said, letting go of her hand. But maybe that wasn't true, perhaps I would have been able to do it, it's just that I wanted to watch João Freitas now that all his pains had vanished. I wanted to watch all of them and wonder: Why did you go away, why didn't you all stay here as I see you now? And only now did I realise that Maria Moniz was there too, but she wasn't dancing, she was sitting to one side beating out the rhythm of the music with her stick and I decided to go and sit with her because I still stuck to my old idea, my conviction that she was me as an old woman and that she had already been me when she was young.

Don't you really feel like dancing? I asked her, sitting down next to her.

Goodness no, she said, not with these swollen legs! I'm happy just to watch my children. Didn't you tell me they were all far off, in America? Certainly, but they've all come back, they're here tonight just to dance the *chamarrita*. So I looked around and thought that it was better to keep words at a distance, because who knows when they were said, even though it seemed that everything was happening now. This was a good moment to mix up time, to let it go and see it flow in that strange way it has—so many little segments destined to remain floating—now that João Freitas was dancing with his wife from the past, and the two Lima sisters who were in California were also here.

Don't be frightened, said Maria Moniz, the only thing that exists is what we see, we're here and we're not here, it doesn't count for much. This is our end-of-summer festival. It must seem incredible to someone like you who comes from far away, but we are used to it. I should tell you that later on there might be a bull fight, but we always have to wait and see until the last minute, we never know if the bull is going to arrive or not. But if it comes it brings good luck. Make a wish to see it, it makes for a great finale.

I don't remember if the bull came or not; I seemed to have waited for it for a long time as I listened to the *chamarrita*, to have seen it and not seen it. A few days later I asked Malvina Sebastião. I said to her: Don't think I'm crazy, but I can't remember anymore if there was a bull or not at the Cabrito festival.

How should I know? she answered. It's years since I've been to festivals like that. It would be torture, the *chamarrita* is irresistible, you just can't watch it without getting up to dance.

I looked up at the darkening sky and I didn't notice that at that very moment Maria Moniz was arriving, walking her slow steps, for she often came to see Malvina Sebastião in the late afternoon, to sit with her for a while on the veranda and look at the sea from another perspective. It was very special, the friendship between them, and very finely balanced: one of them talked all the time, and the other listened all the time with her eyes elsewhere. Malvina Sebastião gave her just enough time to settle herself in the breeziest corner and then started on her as if she was getting into the spirit of a game.

You tell her, Maria, she said loudly, you tell her if the *chamarrita* is irresistible or not!

The other woman kept her eyes looking out to sea, presenting us with her profile of a shining helmet ready for battle.

It's true, it really is true, she replied.

They didn't look at one another, yet I felt coursing between them a deep and playful understanding, and so I said, have it your way ladies; that must mean that it must all have been a night dream and I left them in that lovely ironic complicity of theirs, made up of the long silences of Maria Moniz and the incessant flow of words from Malvina Sebastião.

I really don't remember if the bull arrived or not, but I do remember how I set off back home once the dancing had finished and everyone started to leave, when the night hour together with the sea and its wind had caused the temperature to drop. I lit my way with the torch, listening to time marked out by the powerful waves smashing against the rocks, tasting again the savour of my breathing carried right into the centre of my body with the spicy flavour of a liqueur I had never drunk before, a mixture of honey and sweet smelling flowers.

I didn't even hear his steps behind mine, only when he was close up to me and placed a hand on my shoulder and then instinctively I shone the light into his face.

Did you have a good time? And I answered any words that came into my head, the way I do when I have no time to think before speaking. But it was certainly something neutral, because to answer him properly I would have had to call him by his name, and I didn't know his name, and I certainly couldn't call him Mr Drink.

Did I frighten you?

My goodness, if we had met like this when we first knew each other, maybe, but now I am glad we are going back together.

It's a little chilly, isn't it? Do you want my jacket?

No thanks, it's fine. I didn't notice you there at the festival.

I arrived at the last minute, you see, that's what I always do at the Cabrito festival: I leave it as long as I can and then I miss the best part.

What was the best part this time?

The kid, same as always. When I arrived it was all finished. I hope you had some of it to eat.

I just tasted it. I wasn't hungry.

Not good. So both of us missed the best part. Well, did you like it then?

I would say it was rather strange, even a little sad.

You're right, I think so too. People who have gone away shouldn't come back here on holiday to mix with people who never left in the first place, it just adds heaviness to heaviness.

But you are one of those people. Yes, but I should stop; I should decide either to stay or not come back here at all.

What is it that still ties you to a land so far off from yours?

Would you believe me if I said it is a mystery? I have no wife, I have no children, I haven't even worked for years. Maybe it's because the winters are long here, and very wet, and I've grown old. No, I'm telling you a lie. Do you know what it is about America? It's a monstrous swindle. Now you really will take me for a silly old fool, but in America there are supermarkets as big as small towns, and they are open day and night.

Are you telling me that's why you carry on living over there?

Exactly that. You can't imagine it, but somehow it's very comforting. I do huge amounts of shopping and it keeps me busy for hours on end. I buy a heap of things I don't need and I feel as though I am outside of time, almost happy. I've allowed supermarkets to fill up my life—it's very sad I know, but that's the way it is. It's a whole process, you know? So many bonus points, so many goods for free, more points and you win a trip somewhere, spend more than a certain amount and there's a draw and a bit of free petrol. They really have filled up my life.

Well, take my advice and empty yourself of them again.

I try every year, I stay here for two months and think I'm cured, then I go back over there and everything starts up again in the same frenzy—I walk up and down those aisles as if they were avenues of unimaginable beauty. I've been swindled by America, by all those TV channels that mean I don't have to do anything about my insomnia; I spend my whole life in supermarkets or drinking beer watching sports programmes.

Listen, this isn't a good conversation after a festival like the one we've just been to. You all went to America and it was the wrong thing to do.

We went to work.

Your fathers and your grandfathers didn't do it. You chose change, thinking you were doing right, but you were wrong.

But did you know there was a dictatorship here?

Of course I know.

But maybe you don't know that it was almost worse here than it was in Portugal; here there was a dreadful hunger.

You were still wrong. Sometimes it's worth waiting in order not to lose everything—you wouldn't be telling me about all this nonsense that you have to find to fill up your life with.

You mean: Please, let's not say any more, let's go home in silence, let me think about the sound of the *chamarrita* again.

I offered him my arm and switched off the torch because you could see the lights of Arcos in the distance now. But he said that wasn't right, women never offer a man their arm, he was too much of an old dog to be taught any new tricks, to accept such a revolution, and he offered me his. It really was a lovely walk; the *cagarros* were flying so low in the clear night that we could see the markings on their wings. As we passed in front of the uninhabited priest's house, the plant-man was lying stretched out on the dry stone wall, his arms hanging loosely by his side.

Did you like the table centrepiece you won at the draw? he asked.

Beautiful. It was a present from you, wasn't it?

I know nothing about it. My roots are here; I can't move.

When we arrived back at Arcos, the night was almost finished, the sky was opening up in an endless melting of colour, and the air was vibrating in vertical tremors along the walls of the houses.

I would like to kiss your forehead, Drink said to me. I would like to wish you good night as I would a daughter. Do you mind? He kissed my forehead and then he pressed me into his arms in a hug. You have always meant so much to me, he said, using *tu*, the familiar form of address. Ever since the day you were born, my daughter.

Me too, I answered, because there was no more reasoning to be done that night, and everything went on its own infinite way, to the point of meaninglessness.

We stood there embracing for a moment longer, then we separated and he said, using *lei* once more, Sleep well.

He moved a few steps away, walking towards his house, as

I stood watching him in those movements of an old man. He was half way between where I was standing and his own gate when he turned.

Tell me one thing, he said. Who were you talking to before, along the road?

With the plant-man at the priest's house, I answered.

Did you really see him and hear him?

Certainly, and I think he turned up at the festival at Cabrito, even if he says he never moves because of his roots.

Don't believe him, said Drink, he goes wherever he wants, and whenever the fancy takes him he can transform himself at will. But don't be afraid of him, he's a beautiful soul; he is the angel of Pico.

Chapter ten

Arcos

I f you wish, you can spend day after day without leaving the house. The main thing is not to be in the habit of sleeping too late, because in that case you'd at least need to be up and awake, and to have a good ear. Here at Arcos, between half past eight and nine o'clock in the morning, you see what only in this place would be called a frenetic life.

The first thing is the van of the bakery, *Padaria Lurdes*, a continual honking of the horn which sounds almost like the siren of an ambulance, and applied at or less the same speed, too. Something tells me that this is the mentality of the van itself, an impatience on the part of the motor that wants to see us all in the street by the time it arrives. Either you are there, and ready, or else it doesn't stop and you can't buy bread. It's a waste of time running behind after it, the man driving never looks in the rear view mirror and with one hand he is constantly sounding the horn to the point of deafening himself. If I happened to meet the driver doing anything different, I'm sure I wouldn't recognise him, to the extent that I can see the man as part and parcel of the van itself, the same brownish colour of skin and hair, the shape of his eyes perfectly round like the headlights. He is a man who never laughs, but you couldn't call him sullen. He's a man who drives the van of the *Padaria Lurdes,* whose one real passion is the horn, a high pitched sound like an animal stretching out his neck to listen. He's not the one who sells the bread. Half way down the side of the van it opens up to reveal a girl who is warm and round as a freshly baked roll, who gets fat on the smell of the bread she breathes in. Round her waist she wears a bag full of coins to give people change, and when she has none left she turns to the driver, asking him for whatever she needs. He hands over whatever he is asked for without saying a word, without taking his left hand off the steering wheel.

They sell two types of bread, the soft white one for more delicate palates and the rougher one, heavy and damp, which keeps for days on end. This is the one I buy, and it's not at all a question of taste, it's just that I eat a great deal of it, and that way I don't have to hurl myself down the steps of my house every morning when I hear the horn which sounds like a demented turkey. I buy bread once a week; the other days I watch the van of the *Padaria Lurdes* as it rushes by, the huge cloud of reddish dust that it throws up behind it.

The next man to arrive is the fish-man. I call him that, but it's not always the same man, there are several of them—some of whom are real fishermen, while the others are a bit more make-do. I hear one of them going by just before dawn on his rusty old scooter. He goes up onto the rocks near Cabrito and fishes with a rod. This way he catches nothing but *charros*, small fish, which have a similar shape and flavour to sardines. The first few days I was here I asked him: Do you never catch sardines?

She never gives sardines, he answered, leaving me to work out for myself that 'she' was the sea.

Then he added: On the mainland for sardines.

The real fishermen are the ones who have a boat. When they turn up they come with an open truck and bring enormous fish, though all I buy are a few *imperial* and the occasional *carapau*. They weigh them on old metal scales which lost any colour a long time ago and you have to go into the street with a plate of your own because they don't have any plastic bags for you to take your fish home in.

Whoever it is, the fish-man drives his means of transport very slowly, honks the horn, and then pauses for several seconds before honking again, and during the pauses you can hear his cry echoing along the street, *Peixe, peixe, peixe!*

After that, there is nothing but silence. The person who brings the milk doesn't make any noise. He comes down every day from the mountains with his big, dark red van. He's a tiny man with enormous dark whiskers, kept company by the glinting of his milk containers and the wagging tail of his little dog, Vasquinha. This quiet man neither sounds his horn nor yells out, and he lives alone up in a hut up in the hills. He must have a family: here everybody marries very young and they are also very faithful to each other. On an island as small as this one there is no murder, there is no theft and nobody desires another man's wife. But as you can't take a woman to live up there, he comes down for the weekends, sometimes even just for the day, or for the night, just so as not to feel himself too abandoned by life, and to eat a good meat and vegetable stew at a table with other people instead of just drinking milk and feeding himself with cheese.

He sells a special kind of milk that is almost indigestible. If you let it stand for a while, it forms a thick layer of cream, which tastes strongly of hay. A delicate stomach takes time to get used to a taste like that. The first few days I swallowed it down trying to ignore the wild flavour, but several hours later I still had a strong, heavy taste in my mouth.

If you could happily live on just bread, milk and fish you could avoid going up to Santa Luzia for several days. Now and again João Freitas brings me two or three kilos of potatoes, and when the season is right you can pick blackberries and wild figs. In a thirty-year old guidebook for tourists, I read that the island of Pico was the fruit market of the Azores. That's long gone, the old are dying off and nearly all the young people have gone to America or Canada, the fruit garden is neglected, fruit and vegetables are rare produce even in the few food shops of the larger villages, and like all rare goods, they cost a small fortune. The ugliness of the fruit and vegetables is remarkable; it's the kind of stuff we find on our local markets as they are about to close, thrown into the gutter. Our spoilt lot go around with their plastic bags, fussily poking and prodding, and after all that, all they take is two apples after testing them with their thumb, or a single clump of lettuce after throwing away the outer leaves. They won't take any of the cucumbers—they're too yellow-looking—and they'll only take the peaches after caressing them with their fingers; if the skin crumples, they're left where they are. Our spoilt lot shop with weighty reflection, and buy nothing more than they need for that day; anyway tomorrow there will be as much stuff again on the stalls. Here they would be utterly perplexed; here they sell rotten goods at a high price and the people who can afford to buy it aren't so fussy—they don't stand there turning it over in their hands before putting it on the scales. This isn't locally grown fruit, some comes from the mainland, most from Argentina. People who live here get by with having a small orchard; the tourists get the rotten stuff.

I won't buy rotten goods. I can manage with the potatoes João Freitas brings me and a few cans of tinned syrupy fruit when I take the bus to Madalena. I keep my money so that now and then I can rent a car and go round the island, to go and take a closer look at the volcano, or the roads flanked with enormous bushes of hortensia, or, from a height, to gaze at the great expanse of the *misterios*. They couldn't find another name for these parts left ever more barren by the lava of ancient eruptions. Nothing more can be grown on this land, just a great quantity of wild vegetation which comes up thickly and strongly through who knows what devilish design. Here all you see are trees bent and twisted towards the mountains because of the strong wind coming off the sea. On Pico there are plenty of these *misterios,* it's an island that is constantly changing, you go from sun to shadow within a few metres, from torrid heat to freezing cold when the great ocean clouds descend swiftly and heavily. It's a vivid, almost cheerful and dramatic landscape within a tiny space which seems to be saying: Here one can be born, here where I feel myself at one with spontaneous greenery and abundant flowers, and even over there, amongst the vineyards. But over there, you can see for yourself if you know your own end; over there you can die in peace if you are in peace, or in torment if you are in torment.

Here where I live, at Arcos, on the black volcanic lava where not a blade of grass grows, this should be a place of death if everything had its own allotted place. But instead, this is an island in constant flux, where even death has turned into an unpredictable pilgrim—sometimes it sets out to take the place of life and the glinting of the sun makes the long lava stretch look like a snake at rest, a puppy on its back with its paws in the air, head pointing towards Cachorro and tail towards Cabrito. Here at Arcos is its soft belly where the waves are playful and languid. It's nothing to do with the weather, even when the rain's falling. It is like a reptile, a happy and harmless reptile: at Cachorro it opens its jaws to drink, at Arcos it breathes sweetly with the rapid beating of young hearts, and at Cabrito it wriggles its tail to swish off any insects. Nobody will say so openly, but it's not difficult to grasp that death has gone elsewhere … who knows … maybe to Santo Amaro, or perhaps it's gone down as far as Lajes, it's crossed the mountain pastures covered in mist and now it's over there, draining out the sun. For this is what happens here when good weather and death are thrown together here: the sun lights up and warms as it always does, but it is just pretence, for the real sun has gone off as a shipwreck where there is a storm and there it celebrates the optimism of life.

Now it's really nice here, the people who were here counting the days of their vacation have gone back to the other side of the ocean and taken away with them their gaudy Bermudas and those baseball caps which make their faces look so twisted. I'm talking about the children, not about their parents, for their parents are as glorious as ever, serious and melancholic, never noisy, they only speak in a loud voice if they are drinking, and even then the tone is that of a man calling out at sea and knowing how insignificant a human voice can be when before you is the wave which swells itself up and then breaks half way along its length. Years of distance have left their speech less resonant, and this comes back only with the *vinho de cheiro* and the *angelica*, as they tell the tales of what some of them have been in time to see or which they heard in their childhood.

The fathers of these fathers would go out to sea hunting enormous monsters, the beautiful siren voices coming from the deeps which these men would listen to from their boats, by which they would sometimes let themselves be entranced, nodding their heads in the breeze.

Once upon a time on this island there were twice as many people living here as there are now, Maria Silva told me, but there was also hunger, a great deal of hunger, and that is why so many of them left. And I understand this. I don't judge it so harshly now, it's a tradition of the whole of history to go from one world to another; but it makes me feel very melancholy, as if this tendency to brooding and low spirits was on behalf of those who have never felt it themselves. And I imagine these people setting out with their hearts so full of hope, a hope that empties itself of the past from the very outset of their journey. But we are not that different, and this amnesia of theirs, I know full well, lasts as long as they do not come back, and maybe after years, as if by chance (although chance does not exist) it becomes a real need. I'm going back to see my land, they announce it like that to their friends, as if it were a game that comes back to mind fifteen or twenty years later. You know what I fancy doing? I've got a notion to go back to where I come from, no caravan this year, I'd forgotten that I have a house over there, who knows if it's still standing or if it's been swallowed up by the sea, all of a sudden I want to find out. And then it turns out that when they go back to where they live now, they think about it with belated distress and they wonder, what on earth had happened to me, who was I not to think about it? I see the ones who come back, a real frenzy, they spend all their time working around the abandoned house, making it like new, so that at least it won't feel so alone when winter comes, poor little house of their childhood.

Their children watch them without understanding really what's going on, what's the difference between this holiday and all the others in the past? Let the kids have a good time, let them swim in the sea which is beautiful and calm, but not them, they don't have time. Maybe at the end when they've put right what has been neglected for so long, although when you look at it all they have now is a heavy weight that presses hard against their conscience. Of course I understand them, and in the evening I see them all gathered around the well talking together about the time when everyone went away to drown over there in California, even the memory of youth. The women bring a homemade cake to eat in the freshness of the lovely Atlantic breeze. And there's always someone a bit bolder who has his guitar with him and plays it, inviting them to dance a *chamarrita* from the past. Do you remember this one? The first steps will always be taken by someone who has never left: Look, you do it like this, then this, and this. And then they will all get up and dance, a bit awkwardly, as best they can, trying to sing the words at the same time, because memory is slow and then everything comes back in a rush to devour all the time which has flown away. There will be space enough for a few tears before it's time to go to bed. *Boa noite*, it's been really lovely. It's been old times.

I never join them, of course, that would be to invade a time that was not my own. I would have liked to, but I watch them and that's it. I watch them and in honour of their scattered lives, I vow that I'll never go to America, to that depot of the dead and the dying come from afar, because they are all I would see there, and I would hear the ironic voice which chases them away when they are getting on in years: Go and spit out the sickness which has grown inside you in your own land, there's not much more for you to do here now that you are old. Go away and wallow in the time of your nostalgia, the time of death. But remember that we want you to stay grateful to the end, and on the roofs of your houses, which have been busily disintegrating, alongside the flag of the only country which really belongs to you, make sure that you raise the flag of America, of the country which saw you arriving in rags, destitute, and which gave you more than you hoped for, and have them flutter together for ever.

I watch them dancing the *chamarrita* and I think: My friends, where on earth did you go to, to find Eldorado? A bit *na California* and a bit coming back here, when you've exhausted yourselves over there with searching? Why are you searching for it if it is already in pieces? Sure, the baubles of Eldorado which you carry in your pockets, with your hand ever ready to squeeze them tight when you are overtaken by sadness, and then equally ready to throw them up into the air, just like at Carnival, to the point where you'll be lucky if a tiny fragment of your Eldorado is left to you.

As for me, I have nothing to reproach anyone for, I'm here in your home and I look at you. But I feel like doing exactly the opposite of what all of you did, to emigrate in an unusual and odd way, to come and live here for ever. What would you think of that? The people who never left would understand it. They are men of few words, with never anything to say, they watched you leave without saying anything; they would do the same if they were to see me arriving forever. They are thoughts.

A dog I met at the *minimercado* in Bandeiras has taken to spending most of his time here on my veranda. I've named him Duarte and the last few days he's gone off less and less, only if I go too, and at night he wants to sleep inside the house, stretched out in front of the door, with his nose against the gap beneath the door to sniff the wind. If I were to leave what would you do, Duarte? It's a slightly ridiculous thought, it would soon turn into a legend around these parts—the foreign woman who stayed on the island because of a dog. She could have taken it with her. End of legend. So what on earth was she doing, did she stay as a subtle form of revenge against the emigrants or for love of a four-legged animal? Animal, it's a word that is close to *anima*, soul. My dear little Duartinho, if one day I should ever write something on our story, I would write that one day, somewhere on the roadside near Bandeiras, I found an animal with a beautiful soul which I called Duarte and who became my great friend. Because if you must have a soul, at least let it be a good one, better than mine, otherwise Mr Descartes was quite right when he denied it to you without a second thought.

I'm used to this place by now, to the road-earth-road, to the tip of Pico that is almost always covered in clouds that float down slowly onto it until they make it disappear completely. Up there are the pastures of the island, the little lakes of Caiado and Capitao where the cows are taken to water. It's good to go up there in fine weather, but as is always the case, it's also good to go up there when it's cloudy and the cows and bulls overrun the streets and you suddenly see them appear in front of you, from within a cloud which was resting on the surface of the earth, like the ghosts of ancient animals which welcome you into another time.

If I were to live here, I would like to have a house of my own, but I would like it to be this one, with Mount Pico at its back, with all its green slopes, and with the black lava rocks in front which drop down sheer into the sea.

The family of João Freitas has left; he's the only one still here. There are only two of us non-residents left here now. Every time there are just a few days left of our contract, I ask him to renew it for me for another month and he, in his turn, puts off going back to California. A few days ago, I asked him to leave open the window of that room of his. In the morning I like having my coffee on the veranda and knowing that if I turn to the left I see the ocean, and to the right, over the red road, his lovely statue of the *Bom Jesus Milagroso*. He smiled and headed off towards the well; I saw him lower a glass tied with an old piece of string and have a good early morning drink. I thought to myself it must be the only water he drinks all day, the only flushing out of stomach and intestines which will help to clean out who knows what hardened prostate problem, if it is indeed true that water helps.

You can stay here without noticing the passage of time; the days run swiftly past without interruption. Without anything happening at all, we pass from the morning vans which come to sell us our subsistence food to the darkness of the night, announced by the triple lament of the *cagarros,* which sound so like the wail of a new born baby... I've read all the books I brought from Italy, the only thing for it is to go to Madalena, to a shop that sells practically everything and is called *Bel'Arte,* and buy a book in Portuguese. Just one for now because I haven't a clue if reading is like hearing it spoken by these people whom I know by now. It's a novel by one Dias de Melo, a writer from the Azores who was born right here in Pico, I bought it because I liked the title, *Nem todos tem Natal.* I also liked the cover, which shows a stylised reproduction of the Pico volcano. It starts with these words: *Ti Joaquim Picanco, as pernas a posarem-lhe como dois trambolhos, estas alavancas como que esto a ficar enferrujadas.* With great difficulty, I worked out it was something about an old man with legs like tree-trunks. But it was really hard, and though there were only one hundred and twenty four pages, it was still going to take me a fair amount of time. Reading's another matter altogether, you haven't got the expression of the person talking to help you, the tone of the voice. Some meanings come across through the spoken rhythm; I could get João Freitas to help me, in the mornings, when he goes out for his walk. I could call to him from the window and ask him, What does *enferrujadas* mean? And he would bend down to the ground to pick up something rusty and he would show it to me, scratching his fingernail over the surface, and then he would raise his arms slightly in that particular way of his, elbows against his body and the palms of his hands facing up to the sky, the way he has of suggesting that he doesn't know what else he can say to make himself understood.

You can hardly read a whole book in this fashion; it would become the book of another person, the words of Dias de Melo and the mime of João Freitas. I shouldn't be in a hurry—if there's a word which I don't know, its meaning will be made clear by other words, it will be like a cross reading rather than a crossword. I've all the time in the world.

It seems a peaceful enough relationship, but in fact between me and João Freitas it's a state of war. He's decided that he will go back to America only after I've left; he wants to see me give up. We smile at each other and we do a thousand tiny things for each other: the gas canister hasn't even finished and he brings me another one, he loads it onto his shoulders and I see him climbing up the stairs with the pliers in his trouser pockets. He checks the water cistern to see if there is enough in it, and every time he sees me it's always the same question, Everything all right? Need anything?

Since his family left, I often invite him to dinner. We don't speak much. He tells me I am a good cook but he eats very little, his plate is nearly always still half-full at the end of the meal. His feasting days are over, buried over the *na California*. This must be the fifth or sixth bottle of *angelica* he's given me now, we drink it together after eating, as we watch the night coming over the ocean and wait for the first cries of the *cagarros*. Now and again one of them goes mad, he tells me, they lose their bearings, and end up walking in the middle of the street like lost dead souls. When they go mad they no longer fly, they walk and get run over by cars, poor beasts; you find them in the morning squashed and flattened out of shape, their wings awry and the beak almost always shattered. Their eyes are colourless, the eyes of the blind.

Here there is a high level of humidity. Sometimes I can feel it in my bones: I lift up my left arm and the shoulder blade creaks almost instinctively. The weather changes here ten times a day, the aging damp is dried up an hour later by the sun, and then swept away by the speed of the wind.

Here I play a game that I used to play with my mother: I lie on the ground and look at the clouds which change shape, but with the clouds you get in Italy you have the time to say, it's a dog, now it's a man running. Here you have to be quick, you have to guess, you've hardly had time to say it's a dog and it's already a man running, an eel or a deer. I've become good at it. I play with Duartinho who understands a bit of my language by now. Then, when my eyes are filled with different shapes, I close them, and sometimes I fall asleep.

The other day I said it to him in no uncertain manner. I

looked out of the window and I said, Listen João, we can stay until the weather turns fine again, we can stay as long as you like, for ever even, but let's not fool ourselves, statues are statues, they do not walk and they do not talk.

He gave me a strange nod of the head and a half smile. And watching him as he set off for his morning walk, I answered him in my mind, asking him: But how could you know that almost every night I dream about it coming out of that room and floating towards me?

João Freitas was already the other side of the red road and, without turning, he waved, lifting his arm. It might have been just him saying goodbye, or it might have been his way of saying, That's my secret.

About the author

Romana Petri

Romana Petri was born in Rome in 1955. Her first collection of short stories, *The Blue Prawn*, was published by Rizzoli in 1990; the title story was recently broadcast on Canadian radio. A writer for *L'Unità,* her three published novels have been very well received in Italy, Germany, Portugal and France.

An Umbrian War—Alle Case Venie, published in 1997—has won several literary awards, including the 1998 Rapallo-Carige Prize and the Palmi Prize, and was short-listed for the prestigious Strega Prize.

The fonts used in this book are from the Garamond and Bodoni families

Other works by Romana Petri are published by The Toby Press

An Umbrian War
Other People's Fathers

Available at fine bookstores everywhere. For more information,
please contact *The* Toby Press at www.tobypress.com